A MAN ON A MISSION. A WOMAN WHO WALKS ALONE. TWO PATHS. ONE DESTINY.

John (Snake) Cole, the newest member of Sentinel Security, is working hard to prove he belongs with the team, determined to avenge his predecessor's death. With their enemy within reach, now is not the best time to meet the sexy woman who claims more than his attention.

Samantha Leigh lived her nightmare. Two tours in Afghanistan and she's done. Alone and content on her farm on the Yorkshire Dales, she trains search and rescue dogs.

Snake and Sam didn't expect to find each other. When Sam's demons re-surface, and a child goes missing. Snake must decide who comes first, Sentinel or the woman who just might be his soul mate.

Justice contains sex scenes between mutually consenting adults. Open the door and off with the clothes. Both Sam and Snake use robust language. They swear sometimes.

JUSTICE

SENTINEL SECURITY BOOK 3

ELIZA RENTON

For my mum and dad. No longer here, but I hope you are looking down with pride.

I am grateful to Louise Wilson, who cast her keen eye on an early draft of Justice and Jody Wallace (Mean Kitty Editing for her insightful copy edit. Thanks also to Dar Albert of Wicked Smart Designs for her fabulous cover.

As always, my writing group, The Saturday Ladies Bridge Club, is an ongoing and amazing support. Thank you, ladies.

PROLOGUE

Thirty miles outside Kabul, Afghanistan, Sam slumped against the driver's door of the SUV, traced a line in the dirt with the heel of her boot, and loosened the strap on her protective headgear. The sweat stuck under her chin strap itched, and she'd give her next meal to take the damn thing off, but that would be asking for trouble. Enemy snipers were everywhere, watching, planning their next ambush.

Another day at the office. Clean-up duty, after the latest terrorist insurgence, assisting locals clambering through what the bastards had left of their homes.

Ed, her partner, sometime bed mate, sat in the passenger seat, heaving. A miracle he had anything left in his stomach, seeing as he'd had his head hung out of the window, vomiting almost nonstop ever since they left the village.

"Sorry, Sam. Must have been something I ate."

Or drank last night? Hadn't she warned him to stop drinking? Often, from memory. But, no, he could handle it. Yeah. Her stomach flipped in empathy as another projectile hit the dirt and edged into her peripheral vision. The bomb dog lying across her feet sighed.

Christ, it stank. She covered her nose and mouth with the sleeve of her combat jacket and inhaled. Smoke and blood. A bit on the woodsy side. Lingering. Powerful. A smell that etched deep into your clothing, boots, and skin, but anything was better than the stink of Ed's vomit.

As scents went, Dior or Givenchy were more to her mum's taste. Finding the shiny gift under the tree, a favourite at Christmas. When she got out of this hellhole, she'd stop by duty-free and grab Mum a few boxes. For old times' sake.

"Here, take this." Sam handed Ed a rag and a water bottle. "We've still got a stop to make," she reminded him.

"Okay, okay. For fuck's sake. Take it easy." Ed threw his head out of the open window.

"Can't do much about roads, mate. Next time, think before deciding another one for the road is a smart idea." Make that ten, she added under her breath, but loud enough to hear.

"Don't start, Sam. I told you, it must have been something I ate."

She huffed. She'd been flat out of patience since the start of the week. The final seven days before her time with the unit and the military ended. Common, everyone said, to have the heebie-jeebies. Hope you might be lucky, survive the madness and make it home. Did she even deserve to escape with no scars, physical at least, after everything she had seen and done during this last tour?

"I'll make it up to you, love."

The gentle squeeze of Ed's hand paired with the plea from his round, sad eyes made it impossible to stay mad at him. They were all doing it tough. One drink too many, the easy way to take the edge off the guilt and pain gnawing through your gut every hour of every day.

"Yeah, yeah." Sam smiled. Not the easy smile of her teens, but the one that offered solidarity.

They'd been seeing each other for six months, snatching any opportunity to be intimate. Pretend. Sober Ed had kept her sane, a caring twat who helped her make it through the day. They'd agreed to date once they were home. See where life took their relationship.

On a good night, lying in her bunk, she imagined a dozen way he might propose.

"Hey, where are you going? This isn't the way to Base. You should have veered west, two clicks back."

Beam me up, Scotty. "Remember, I said we had to make a stop."

"Are you serious? That Afghani kid can wait."

The dog in the back barked. Sam reached over and patted her K9's snout. "Easy, boy. Ed's uber grumpy today." She tossed the dog's empty water bowl into Ed's lap. "Sorry, this won't take long. Use this if you have to chuck. Don't mess up the vehicle. It's unlikely we'll come this way again before the end of the week. Have a nap." One of the younger boys in the village loved chocolate, and she'd promised to bring him Smarties, his favourite, before she left. All day she'd kept them in the cooler, hoping they wouldn't melt.

It didn't surprise her Ed didn't want to stop. He found most adults hard to read. Children? Impossible. On patrol, she happily dealt with the kids while he swore her trust in little people would get her killed one day.

And as soon as she pulled up at Arash's, a chill shivered through her. Since her plane had first landed here six months ago, nothing had felt right. Rather than dwell on how shit-awful human beings were to each other, Sam blamed her unease on the unrelenting heat.

Arash ran around outside the small hut, waving a stick, almost as big as him, slashing it through the air as if it were a sword. Wings flapping, a chicken chased him, squawking its battle cry.

"Stay here," Sam commanded.

Ed groaned and reached for the water bowl. Her dog grunted. Neither prepared to argue. Sam swiped her hand across her forehead, feeling guilty. She'd opened her mouth to apologise for making them wait in the heat when Esin, Arash's mother, flew out of their hut waving an AK47 in one hand, a grenade in the other, yelling as she charged straight at them.

Sam understood limited Pashto, but she had heard these words too many times in the last months. "Death to the infidel." Weeks earlier, Arash's father, a suspected terrorist, had died during a raid by British troops.

Gunfire. The ping of bullets zinged off the surrounding debris, and Esin kept screaming. Fear blocked Sam's throat, refusing to let her take a full breath as her world blew apart.

"Arash, get down." She dashed towards the boy.

"What the hell? Are you out of your mind?" Ed flung the door open.

He made it to the front of the vehicle before a hail of bullets hit him. On impact, his body arched, and his legs crumpled. Her name—the last word on his lips.

"No!" Denial couldn't save him.

Surrounded by a cloud of circling sand, teeth bared, tears streaming down her face, Esin sank to her knees and pulled the pin of the hand grenade. Arash charged towards her and Esin scooped him into her arms. Shut inside the SUV, Bounce was having a mental breakdown, barking to be set free.

Helpless, sucked into a paralysing vortex, Sam's hands hung limply by her side as Arash and Esin spiralled away from her. She closed her eyes and waited for death. The deafening blast sent her somersaulting to the SUV.

The back of her throat on fire, her voice hoarse, she saw no point in shouting. All over. Finished. Arash and his mother were gone.

"Ed?" So many questions, but her partner stared straight through her.

Ed, Esin, Arash, all dead. Drowning in fucking Smarties, Sam sobbed.

CHAPTER ONE

Three years later, Sam stared out of the tiny window of the plane, en route for Mali, wishing she hadn't been a bloody tight-arsed and had booked business rather than cattle class on Air Maroc.

It would have made more sense to accept the military flight, but as a civilian, her active duty days behind her, her purse whined each time she ventured over the budget line. Travelling commercial put her further away from shit she preferred to forget.

Figuring she'd sleep most of the way, she'd chosen the window seat and seriously underestimated how many times a person needed to pee during a three-and half-hour flight. Uncomfortable, Sam shifted her the safety belt away from her painfully full bladder.

As soon as their flight left the Casablanca stop-over, the elderly couple, spread over the two seats to her left, had scoffed their dinner, masked up, and disappeared under their airline blankets. An occasional grunt confirmed they weren't dead. They certainly had stronger bladders.

Next to them, across the aisle, the 'too many drinks at the airport' plonker snored at a pitch that overrode her noise-cancelling headphones.

She could escape to peace in the loo, but then her foot might slip as she leapt over nan and grandad and waking them bordered on sacrilegious. Call her mean, but she didn't want to be their entertainment for the rest of the trip.

Well and truly stuck, Sam sucked in a deep breath and dug in for another episode of *Strike Back*. The last one cracked her up when Stonebridge removed a bullet with the casing still attached from Scott's leg. *Nice one.*

"Get in there, lads," she encouraged, raising her fist at the screen.

"Can I get you something to drink?" Small tray in her hand, the flight attendant peered over the sleeping beauties.

"No, thank you." Another vodka tonic was certainly tempting, but wobbling along the airbridge to meet her employers didn't sit in the 'good look' column.

Sam turned her head to focus on the sun peeking through the clouds. Still some distance away, Africa's terrain drew closer to the aircraft's underbelly. Not much longer before they landed.

An hour later, bladder unemptied, Sam kicked her second suitcase onto the trolley and staggered through the auto doors into Mali's International Airport. Miraculously, she could still take a deep breath without accident.

The pale blue berets of the UN Peacekeeping forces weren't hard to spot in the crowd. Head and shoulders towering over the soldiers, the man in the middle of the small group, officer written all over him, strode her way.

He looked her over, a sleazy smirk covering his face. No doubt in a huff because headquarters sent a woman to train the new K9 handlers. She and her dog, Bounce, were under contract, hired to establish training protocols and guidelines before the UN dogs arrived. And wouldn't you know it, the twenty-first century, and chauvinism still permeated the ranks.

"Good evening. Ms Leigh?" the officer said. The sneer in his voice matched the smirk on his face.

Sam nodded and glued the arm accustomed to saluting strongly to her side.

"I'm Lieutenant-Colonel Routledge." He held out a white-gloved hand, bright enough to blind. "Did you have a comfortable flight?"

Sam pushed the hair out of her eyes and rose to her full height. "Fine, thank you, sir." Sam shook his hand. "Please call me Sam," she added, kicking herself for acknowledging his rank. "I scored an upgrade. Slept most of the way." An unnecessary lie, but it helped her feel in control of a boundary. "Sorry I'm late. The plane got delayed leaving Casablanca, plus we ran into a thunderstorm —turbulence."

Routledge blinked once and waved at the exit. His gaze dropped to her trolley. "Where is your dog? Bounce?"

"On a more direct flight." As he showed no interest in the reason, she didn't offer any. "I will pick her up tomorrow."

"No need. I will send one of my men." The officer turned to the smaller man hovering a step behind him. "See to it, Corporal."

Later, for that conversation. Sam had no intention of letting anyone else meet Bounce in the morning. Eager to get to her quarters, check out her notes for tomorrow's training, she followed Routledge. She had two weeks, not a lot of time, and they needed to get through a ton of information before she returned to the UK.

Too tired to remain abreast with the chauvinist dick beside her, she settled two steps behind and let him lead the way to the car park. His corporal insisted on pushing the luggage. Fine by her. The trolley rattled over the concrete, exacerbating her dim but persistent headache.

Sam crawled into the backseat of the military SUV, praying it had air conditioning, and left Routledge to oversee the loading of her gear. Her eyelids drooped and she must have drifted off because the next thing she knew, they were pulling up outside a hotel. The Splendid. The name blazed across the front of the modern building. Upmarket and pricey if the sweeping driveway and uniformed doorman were any clue. "I thought I'd be staying at the barracks?"

"No, Miss Leigh. You will be much more comfortable here. Give your name at Reception. We have paid the bill for your stay, including your meals." He nodded at the corporal offloading her bags. "He will pick you up at seven o'clock tomorrow morning. *A bientot.* Have a good evening, Miss Leigh."

The Lieutenant Colonel leaned across her lap and opened the door. A simple gesture, but she felt the toe aimed squarely at her arse. Rude, but she was too tired to care. She was up the stairs and checking in before they drove away.

Sam grabbed her room key, grateful when the porter snatched her bags and headed for the lifts. Hell, she needed the bloody loo. Inside her room, she urgently tipped the porter and charged for the bathroom.

Job done, feeling much more human, Sam sat on the edge of her bed and studied the room service menu. Aside from the peanuts and a packet of cheese and biscuits, she hadn't eaten since leaving London, but her eyes were too tired to keep open long enough to decipher the hieroglyphics.

Lying in bed, she hoped Bounce had plenty to eat, that she didn't go out of her mind locked in her cage. Her dog seldom left her side. Not that Sam needed to worry. The ever-capable Kate had made sure didn't miss her flight flight. But Sam fell asleep missing her slobbery kisses.

As planned, the alarm blasted at 6.30 a.m. sharp. Excited to see Bounce, she pulled over the sheet, struggled out of bed, showered, and dressed in record time. Afraid she'd be late getting to the airport, she skipped breakfast and headed out of the hotel, listening to her stomach growl in protest.

It took half a second to call Routledge and have the corporal pick them up later from the hotel. The airport wasn't far from the hotel, and after the long flight, Bounce needed the exercise.

Luckily, Mali's airport was busy, but not huge. It didn't take long to complete the required paperwork and locate the collection area.

Sam knelt and opened Bounce's cage, quickly forgiving her for not waiting for the command to show the love. "Yes, yes, I'm glad to see you too, girl." She scrubbed her behind the ears, Bounce's favourite spot. Her silky fur felt great under her fingers. "Come on, girl. I bet you need a run before work this morning."

By the time they made it to the hotel, grabbed her gear, they were at least half an hour late. Uniform pressed to a knife's edge, the corporal stood to attention by the SUV.

"Good morning, Miss Leigh. I trust you slept well. Lieutenant Colonel Routledge has given me your itinerary." Before she could apologise, he'd opened her door and once again zeroed in on her bags. "We have a full day ahead of us. I hope you had breakfast."

Amazing. He didn't stop for air. Overnight, her driver had turned from mute to motor-mouth. At the mention of a meal, Bounce sniffed the corporal's hand. Not impressed, he snatched his fingers from her curious nose. Sam thrust her leg forward and nudged away Bounce's slobbery tongue and did her damndest not to laugh. "Bounce. Leave it."

The corporal tilted his face to the sky. "*La pluie arrive.* It's going to rain."

"*Non,*" she replied, wondering why he had switched to French. January fell in Mali's dry season. "*Je pense que ce n'est inhabituel pour la période de l'année.*"

He blinked, obviously surprised she spoke French even if her accent sounded naff. "*Vraiment.* Not usual for this time of year."

"*Allons-y. Il n'y a pas de temps a perdre.* No time to waste." Inside, she smiled and watched the corporal's mouth open and close in sync with Bounce's wagging tail. Her tongue lolled at the side of her mouth, offering a doggy grin as Sam opened the door to the back and signalled for her to hop into the SUV. They had work to do.

With a sulky shrug, the corporal sat and started the engine. *Good boy.* Sam turned and winked at Bounce.

With no more chat from the corporal or car radio to distract her, she focused on the passing traffic and running her checks for the day. The airline had delivered the training gear directly to the barracks, making it much easier for her to get straight to work as soon as they arrived. With any luck, the corporal's odd attitude didn't signal more fun to come.

CHAPTER TWO

Cooped up in the Land Rover, Snake swiped at the stagnant air hanging over his head and swatted the umpteenth insect determined to have him for breakfast. He'd forgotten how many trips Sentinel had made to Mali, but dry or rainy season, the flies drove him fucking nuts. Used to tuning shit out, George, Sentinel's K9 lay across the back seat, paws cupped over his ears, snoring. Snake should learn from his dog and catch up on a nap while they waited.

January, technically, in Africa, was the coolest time of the year, but still above 30C this early in the morning. At least the boss had the sense to park under the shade of an acacia. Spanner and Doc pulled in behind them.

This last job was a bloody nightmare. Sanctioned by the French government, Sentinel had carried out a covert rescue of a highly connected finance broker. After securing his release, he whined for a full forty-eight hours until they finally handed his arse over to the French embassy. Ecstatic at having the knob'ed off their hands, his kidnappers were still partying.

Daniel Knight, Sentinel's boss, only agreed to them undertaking the rescue because he planned on combining the trip with locating Seckou, Sentinel's nemesis.

Back when they had been in active service, the team had made it their personal mission to annihilate the terrorist who killed Mike, Sentinel's original comms man and George's handler. After his death, Snake had taken on Mike's role and dog. Big shoes to fill.

Despite local intel pinning Seckou leaving Burkina and crossing the border into Mali, they'd had shit luck locating him. Again. The bastard would give the Scarlet Pimpernel a run for his money.

Snake glanced across the street. Eight hundred hours. Early, but a halo of blinding sun reflected off the glass façade of the ex-pat hotel. He wasn't the only one glad to be going home today, but before they got the hell out of bumfuck Mali, headed to Ouaga and the plane home, they had to pick up his teammates' women. Kate, Doc's wife. Crystal, Spanner's partner, and a friend of Lily's.

Home. Snake rubbed his palms together and closed his eyes. *Soon.* An entire weekend with nothing to do but eat, drink, and fuck. Throw in the Sky Sports channel—heaven. *Bring it on.* For the hundredth time, he recrossed his booted feet on the dashboard.

A car backfired. Snake scrubbed his forehead and cursed the downer of a morning. Made worse by the lack of fucking coffee and sleep. Shit. The whiny Frenchman must have rubbed off on him.

Next to Doc, he took pride in being the most laid-back member of the team. Not much worked his nerve, but he had a thing for punctuality. The girls were late, and it drove him nuts. He needed a plan to execute before his head spun out of control.

"What time did you say Kate expected us, boss? I'm starving." He patted his stomach, not really expecting any sympathy from Knight. During one cocked-up special op, the boss had endured six months of enemy torture, and Snake would bet his last paycheck edible food didn't feature big as must-have for a Taliban prisoner.

Suck it up. That's what he should do, but ever since he'd gotten out of bed, a nagging voice in his head had insisted shit was going down. He rested an elbow on the edge of the half-open window and checked the side mirror for any sign of drama.

Nothing, nada, zip.

Once the girls showed, he'd feel less irritable. Kate was good for a laugh, especially when she hassled Knight, and Crystal didn't know the meaning of a bad day. The woman glowed, although this past month she hadn't seemed as carefree. None of his business. Keeping the woman happy lay squarely on Spanner's shoulders.

Pity Lily, Knight's wife, hadn't made the trip. Last time they had been in Africa, she'd saved his life. He owed her. Without her quick thinking, he'd be brown bread, dead. A long stint in rehab meant he hadn't thanked her, and this trip she'd stayed in London with their new daughter, Mary.

From the photos Knight flashed whenever they stopped to take a breath, the kid looked amazing. A shiny bundle of uncomplicated newness. Good thing Snake didn't have kids. After literally being dumped on a doorstep at two years old, he didn't think he'd have the strength to leave them, not even for a mission.

And that, my man, is why you are single. Fatherhood carried the big R tag. Responsibility. Parents needed to be around for kids, and he had a long list of things to take care of before that could happen. If ever.

Last night, after mission de-brief, he'd taken Elise, from the French team, up on her offer of a nightcap. They had hooked up a few times in London. An expert in tension release, she knew the score. Unlike his team brothers and their women, he and Elise weren't looking for the one and only.

Great tits. Snake drummed his fingers on the top of the steering wheel and chuckled. Hot sex should have been the perfect antidote for the adrenaline tiger gnawing at his gut. "What's holding them up, boss? I thought you said..."

"For fuck's sake." Knight lurched forward, pushed his cap back off his forehead, and squinted at the passing convoy of trucks, cars, and motorcycles. "You are driving me nuts, crying into your shirt one minute, cackling the next."

Knight kicked his boot. "I swear it's worse than travelling with Mary. At six months, she has an excuse. Next time you ride with Doc. If you've got nothing better to do, go grab us a coffee from the hut across the street."

On command, the shutters rattled, officially open for business.

"No sugar in mine," Knight added and pulled the cap back over his eyes.

"Sure," Snake muttered, but didn't budge. Instead, he tapped the air-con button.

They should have left Mali and been well on the road to Ouaga airport an hour ago. Before it got dark and travelling at night became risky. Nothing they couldn't handle, but with women on board, they had planned to make it over the border, and stop for the night. Take turns keeping watch.

"Hey, Snake, you horny git. If you'd slept last night instead of getting all amorous with Elise, you wouldn't need coffee." Doc's voice rang in his earpiece.

Smug bastard. "Fuck off. Don't tell me you haven't got similar plans in mind for you and Kate tonight. I bet…"

Knight nudged his elbow. "Bottle it, the pair of you. Here they come."

About bloody time.

Kate and Crystal stood on the steps leading from the hotel. No sign of Lily's friend. The one he'd met at the boss' wedding. The dog trainer. George liked her shepherd, Bounce. The canine mind-reader lolling on the back seat barked. *Roger that.*

If Snake remembered right, she'd been in Mali training handlers to work with explosive detection dogs for UNOPS, United Nations Office of Public Service. She must be ace at her job.

Knight tapped the horn. Crystal waved. Glad they were finally getting underway he might as well make himself useful. "Open up the boot, boss. There isn't much luggage. Let's load and roll."

"I thought Sam was with them?" Doc asked, already out of the other vehicle, his eyes locked on the redhead striding straight for him, *come to bed* written all over his soppy face. "Long time, no see, sweetheart?" Doc slung his arm around Kate's shoulder.

Knight leaned out of the window. "She is," he confirmed.

Snake sighed. Sam, the invisible woman. *Great.*

Crystal made her way to the other vehicle, where Spanner pulled her in for the full dip and kiss.

Happy-slappies all round. Half their fucking luck. "Not missing each other much, then?" Snake grumbled. Marriage wasn't for him, but lately he'd wondered what it might mean to venture past a one-night stand. At thirty-six, he put it down to a creeping midlife crisis.

"Free." Snake opened the back door to let George out, giving the command for his canine partner to do the necessaries before they got cracking. Disinterested, the dog sat at his feet, lifted his nose in the hotel's direction, and whined. "What's up, boy? Do your thing. We're not stopping once we get started."

Kate half-turned and stroked his arm. "Good morning, Snake, I'm sorry we're late. Sam didn't arrive at the hotel until late last night and overslept."

"No problem." He smiled through gritted teeth. "Hop in. We'll take care of these." He pointed to the bags. Nonplussed, George stared at the entrance to the hotel. Didn't budge, not even for the added incentive of a scratch to the back of his ears. "Home soon, boy." They both deserved a break.

"Does Sam need help?" he asked, doing his best to keep the snark out of his voice.

Kate peered over her shoulder. "Should be right behind us. She must have forgotten something."

Yeah. Like a watch.

CHAPTER THREE

"I'll see if Sam needs help." Snake offered, busting to get them moving.

"Yeah. Time to go." Knight nodded at the hotel.

No shit. "On it, boss."

The Splendid Hotel teemed with people, but at six foot four, seeing over heads rarely posed him any problem. In no time at all, he spotted Sam standing by the lifts. He raised a hand to get her attention, same time as she turned and their gazes locked. Impressive. ESP —next level situational awareness.

Short and slim, her long brown hair danced over her narrow shoulders. Calling the colour of the long mane 'brown' didn't do it justice. The curtain of gold and auburn lights reminded him of falling autumn leaves.

"Hey, Sam." Hoping to speed things along, he dodged the couple in front of him, pushed forward, and got within three feet of her when the unmistakable spit of AK-47 rifle fire ripped through the lobby. His blood ran cold. Shit fell apart. People screamed, split, and ran for their lives.

Both hands flew to protect his head from the glass ricocheting from the mirrors lining the lobby walls. Sam took off, heading for a little girl standing next to the bullet-ridden door to the pool. Frozen to the spot, thumb in her mouth, she stared at the dead woman at her feet.

"Get down!" He could swear she heard him but didn't stop running. Steady on her feet, her boots hopped skilfully over the bloody carpet of injured bodies.

Bollocks. Snake tapped his crackling ear piece. "Boss? You there? Tell me again why terrorist fuckers love lighting shit up."

"Pretty? We're on our..." Knight's voice turned to static as a dozen more men armed with assault rifles and waving nine millimetre pistols flooded the lobby. Terrified people searched for shelter, but the poor bastards were shit out of luck. The large open area, ripe for picking off the enemy.

Snake ducked behind a column, hurled himself into the air, and collided with Sam. His elbow crunched beneath him as they crashed onto the marble floor. Behind him, George yelped.

"Stay down. Don't move," he mumbled against her ear, praying she heard him over the shrieks of panic. Her breaths were short and choppy. "Are you hurt?" he asked, bile rising in the back of his throat.

"No, but you're sodding heavy."

Right then. "Sorry. It's me, Snake, Lily's friend. Be quiet, stay still. I'll get us out of here." Gunfire popped close by, and a teenage boy fell to his knees and clutched his throat. Underneath him, her body trembled and heaved. *Shit.* "Don't vomit." He raised his arm to his face and braced.

"You neither. Get the hell off me."

Ballsy. He didn't mind that, until suddenly she stopped wriggling, and his breath hitched. The woman underneath him felt tiny, easy for a big man to smother. He slowly eased his weight onto his forearms.

"George. Come." He called for his dog.

Nothing. "George." Snake said, louder this time, a sinking feeling in his gut. He scanned the chaos for his partner and dry retched.

George lay on his side, eyes closed, one of his back legs drenched in blood.

No, no, no. "Easy boy. I'm coming." They had to get out fast. The rest of the team would be hellbent on making sure their women were out of harm's way, so until they returned for them, he and Sam were on their own.

He reached for his weapon and cursed. Back on the front seat of the Land Rover. Thank God for the knife concealed in his ankle sheath. Any attacker who got close wouldn't live long enough to regret it.

George whimpered. Snake needed to check on him, but no way could he leave the woman wriggling under him, teasing parts of his anatomy that had no fucking business taking interest.

"Hang in there, boy."

A single bark answered.

In the distance, sirens wailed. Disoriented, Sam closed her eyes. Black dots darted across her eyelids. A dog whined. Glass shattered, walls cracked. *Fuck.* She should be dead.

The unmistakable smell of blood and gunfire gnawed at her gut. A cough ripped through her chest, causing havoc in her tortured lungs. More gunfire. She skimmed her nose across the marble floor, searching for the closest exit? To her right, a shoe bounced off a cracked flowerpot and landed in front of her.

Blood. Sticky crud oozed from the corner of her eye, and in a heartbeat, the shifting sand dunes of the Afghani desert lurched before her, and her stomach took a deep dive.

This is not then. This is not the same. Her shrink's words were no help. Around her, things were going bang. A split second before everything went crazy, she'd spotted the kid. Obviously lost, the child had been within a few steps of her when the shooting started, and something heavy crashed into her.

Arms tucked against her ribs, she inhaled deeply and tried to budge the weight pinning her to the floor. It moved, so not concrete—a mangled corpse?

Her head, the only free part of her body, strained to take in a three-sixty of the foyer. "Shit. They're attacking the hotel." She blinked furiously at the blood threatening to close her right eye.

"Uh, huh? Are you hurt? It's me, Snake, Lily's friend. Help is on the way."

His weight eased slightly on her back.

"George. My dog. He's injured," he continued, the fear in his voice palpable.

She understood. Many times, she'd worried more for the dogs than herself. "I'm okay. Check him."

"No, can't leave you."

"Oh, for fuck's sake. Go, hero. I'm having trouble breathing with you on top of me." Grateful that the shooting had stopped, for now, Sam humped her shoulders, dug her elbows into her sides, and tried again to heave him off her.

With any luck, after causing maximum carnage, the terrorists weren't game to hang around for the gendarmes.

"I'm Lily's friend," he grunted.

"Yeah, Snake, so you said. Go. Check your dog."

"Stay there. I'll be right back." Finally, he rolled off her, allowing much needed air to make it to her lungs and went to his dog. "Stay," he repeated.

"Sorry, no can do. I have to catch the bus that just pulled up."

Snake squinted at her as though she were hallucinating. No such luck.

Sam gently patted around her eye. The blood dripped from a cut above her eyebrow. Rolling her lips together, she inched over to join Snake. Slumped against a crumbling column, he cradled his dog's head in his lap.

His long legs stretched in front of him, well over six-foot and solidly built, ex-military written all over him. But he looked like a little kid with the bluest eyes she'd ever seen glistening with tears. She gulped at the seriously sad sight, and her heart swelled with a whole heap of shit she didn't need. Not now. Never again.

"Hey, let me look." She stretched her fingers towards the dog's nose for a sniff and immediately backed off at his owner's rumbled warning. No one touched his animal.

"I have some experience. He's injured his hind leg." Stating the bloody obvious worked. He eased his hold, allowing her to move closer, but he never took his eyes off her.

"Hey, feller." The lump in the back of her throat grew as she feathered her fingers over the top of the dog's head.

"George, his name is George."

"Hey, George. Steady, boy." Swallowing hard, she kept her breath even as she took his paw into her palm. Smashed to beetroot. Not much chance he'd keep the hind leg. Luckily, she didn't see any other injuries.

"He's going to be okay." Her voice sang with Pollyanna sunshine as she gently touched the back of Snake's bloodied hand.

"Don't fucking bullshit me." Snake gulped, his bottomless gaze boring into her.

"Fair. Okay, he's badly hurt. We need to get the hell out of here, and your dog to a vet, before he bleeds to fucking death. Better?"

A single nod.

"Okay, hold him steady while I tourniquet the leg." Used to working with K9s, Sam never left home without a rag or two in her pocket. She pulled out several and bound George's leg tight. If she could slow the bleeding, he might have a chance.

Snake lifted his head, and she quickly glanced away, unable to reassure him more than she already had.

"Thanks, Sam. You okay?" The deep voice suited his giant size.

"Yeah. I'm fine. Not my first visit to hell." Her last trip to Satan's playground had been with Ed. She rubbed her eyes and winced as her fingers scraped the cut. They burned from the thick, acrid smoke piling into the lobby.

26

War. No one won. Done with the military but unable to sever the bond completely, back home she had set up her kennels. First Oxford, now the Yorkshire Dales. Trained dogs to detect explosives and find bodies. A weird combo.

George whined, snapping her straight back to the present shitstorm. "Snake, we need to move. Now. Can you carry your dog?"

"Yeah." Cradling George in his arms, he anchored the whimpering bundle to his torso. One push from his tree trunk legs and he climbed to his feet.

"Got a gun?" Sam asked.

"Nope. In the Rover." He aimed his nose at what used to be the door to the street. "A knife. My ankle." With a sniff, he shoved his right foot forward.

"Great." Thankful, she rolled up his pant leg and retrieved the knife. Up close combat had never been her preferred mode of engagement, but she'd take it over dying. "Stay behind me." Head on a swivel, she clenched Snake's knife in front of her and made her way through the bodies and broken—everything.

Outside, the shock of the fresh air hitting her lungs started her coughing. Grateful she hadn't had to use the knife, she swiped her sweaty palm on her pants. Behind her, Snake spluttered. *Damn.* She hadn't thought to check him for injury. "Here, give me your dog." She held out her arms and nodded at George.

"No." He swayed, and she steadied his elbow. "It's okay. I've got him. We need a vehicle."

Full of bright ideas. Like every military man she'd ever met. *Easy, Sam. He's in shock.* Though he'd never admit it. Terrified of losing his dog. She got it. Over to the right, she spotted a beat up lorry with a couple of goats in the back.

No use arguing over who carried the dog. Focussing ahead, Sam picked her way over the crumbling hotel steps and made a beeline for the lorry, trusting Snake to follow.

CHAPTER FOUR

Snake held George in his arms, the dog he considered family as Knight opened the door to the hotel room they had stayed in last night. The boss took one look at him and Sam and turned ghost white. His arms shaking, Snake pushed past him and lay his dog in the nearest chair.

Sam's eyes followed him as she did her own duck and weave to dodge Crystal's open arms and failed. Her chin fell heavily on Cry's shoulder, and his gut tightened, wishing he could be the one offering Sam support. Heaven knew she deserved it.

Cool. Despite the devastation, she'd stopped George from bleeding out back at the Splendid. Her soft, capable assertion everything would be okay had calmed them both. He tried to catch her eye and failed.

After leading them out of the hotel, Sam easily hotwired the lorry, ignored the bleating goats, and drove faster than a Valkyrie in heat to get them out of there. He sure as shit hated feeling helpless. Useless. She wanted to go straight to the vet, but as much as he cared for George, he insisted on joining the others. He wanted Sam safe.

Lily had mentioned she'd served. She sure handled herself as well as any soldier. For such a small package, she commanded every atom of space around her, shone brighter than any beacon. That cut above her eye looked angry. Had to hurt.

"Doc, check Sam's eye." He swore under his breath when she shrugged. If his arms weren't full of injured canine, he'd make sure she let Doc take care of her. Sam waved off his concern but didn't object when Crystal lowered her onto a seat by the small window.

Knight finished his call and strode to the door, rattling the key to the Land Rover. "No one get comfortable. Lieutenant Colonel whatsit…"

"Routledge," Sam offered, raising her eyes to the ceiling.

"That's him." Knight nodded.

"Any help?"

"Not so as you'd notice, but he assures me they have everything under control. Though, under the circumstances, I'm having a hard fucking time visualising what that means. Anyway, he doesn't have to tell me twice our services are not required. We are good to go."

"Anybody claimed responsibility yet?" Spanner asked, his hand gliding over Crystal's back.

"No. Too early for the fuckers to decide who gets kudos. You and Snake take care of George. The rest of us will keep going to Ouaga and meet you at the villa. Doc. Is Sam okay to travel?"

Doc patted Sam's eye, and she flinched. Belly on fire, Snake lurched to his feet. "Don't hurt her," he growled.

"Easy, knob'ed. Sam's fine. Take care of George." Doc didn't even look at him.

"Stand down, Snake. I'm fine." The tips of Sam's fingers rested on his forearm and his world shifted one-hundred-and-eighty degrees, righted itself at the warmth of her touch. The cut above her eye oozed blood, and she looked anything but fine.

"Do as Knight says and take care of your dog. It's chaos out there, but the vet won't have left the UN post. He will help."

George sniffed the air and whimpered. "Hang in there, boy. We'll soon have you fixed up. Double bones tonight." Outside, Snake slid the dog into the back seat of the SUV, closed the door, and climbed in next to Spanner.

He didn't pray, but he always hedged his bets, so he closed his eyes and gave it a shot.

George suffered when he became distracted. The Sentinel team watched each other's backs, and that included their canine. And he'd botched it.

The rag Sam had tied around George's leg leaked blood and his mate didn't whimper. Only the shallow rise and fall of his chest said he lived. So far. "Step on it, Spanner."

"Talk to me, Sam. How are you feeling?"

Doc sat next to her in the back seat, his voice echoing in the space she tried to reach but couldn't. Straining to hear him made her headache worse. Why did he expect a coherent answer when words insisted on staying planets away from her mouth? Lost in Afghanistan along with Ed and Arash. *Same sounds, different dead people.*

A hand fluttered in her side vision. Kate reached for her arm. Startled, Sam flinched and clasped her trembling hands together in her lap. No comfort, not yet, even if Kate understood. A couple of years ago, she and Doc had barely escaped being killed in a bomb explosion, but she couldn't handle one more caring smile, another sympathetic sigh.

Hell! Her eyelashes were heavy with tears, ready to spill over her cheeks. Her bottom lip stung from the sharp dig of her teeth. Exhausted from Doc's prodding and poking, she wanted to disappear.

Thank God Bounce had made it to the airport before the attack. "George?" she croaked. "How's he doing?"

"No word yet. Snake will be in touch, hun." Crys turned and offered a tissue.

"Thanks." Goosebumps erupted on her forearms. "Shit. I'm going to be sick. Pull over."

Knight swerved, the sudden move throwing her hard against the SUV's metal door.

Before he fully stopped, she'd flung open the door and puked. "I'm sorry."

"Hang in there Sam. We're almost there." Voice steady, Doc's hand pressed lightly between her shoulder blades, his voice calm. "Head between your knees, that's a girl."

Beads of cold sweat broke out on her forehead. She brushed her sleeve across her mouth, shook off Doc's hand, and staggered to her seat.

"Drink, Sam. No more talking." Kate handed her a bottle of water and finally snared her fingers.

Knight chuckled. "You tell her, Doc."

The skin beneath her eye twitched, but thanks to whatever drugs Doc had pumped into her at the hotel, the rest of the journey faded into a blur. Exhausted, she gave up the struggle to keep her eyes open and fell into the darkness.

"We're here, Sam." Kate shook her back to reality, climbed out of the vehicle, and offered her hand.

Lily had mentioned Knight's villa, but surrounded by a tall brick wall and iron gate, Sentinel's headquarters in Africa were much bigger than she'd imagined.

"Sit, everyone, and I'll make us a cup of tea," Crystal offered as soon as they were inside.

"Thanks. You know where everything is. Kate, Sam, we'll be back in a minute. Doc, with me," Knight directed.

Doc checked her pulse before he followed the boss. Immediately, the hairs on Sam's forearm bristled. Used to being a part of the action, it felt odd being side-lined to the sofa.

"Where are they going?" she asked.

"The War Room, hun," Crys returned from the kitchen. Judging from Kate's heavy sigh, their men disappearing behind that particular closed door was nothing new.

"Welcome to the club, Sam. Men gotta do what men gotta do." She huffed. "My guess, they'll be checking in with Snake and George."

Kate's palm rested on her shoulder. Her gentle squeeze sent the damn boulder rolling to the back of Sam's throat. As a kid, her grandfather had given her a stray puppy he found on the dump site. Ever since, dogs had been by her side. A vital part of her life. "He may not survive. I did my best, but he's lost a great deal of blood."

Kate's eyes roamed the room, looking anywhere but at her.

Shit. When would she learn? Truth was not always for the best. "Sorry, I hope he does, but I don't want you to get your hopes up. How long has Snake had his dog?" she added, scrambling for a distraction.

"A couple of years. He was my brother's dog."

Floor, open, and swallow me now. The tendency to speak, before thinking, habitually flung her headlong into trouble. She had gone in with her boots on, route-marched all over Kate. "I'm sorry, I forgot..."

"No need to apologise. Let's think positive." Kate raised a fist and weakly tapped the top of her head. "Touch wood. George will be okay."

Sam barely noticed when Crys returned with a tray of cups and tea. No stranger to adrenaline fatigue, unable to get the little girl at the hotel's frightened face out of her head, Sam trembled as she reached for the sugar.

"Here, hun, let me," Crystal pleaded. "I remember. Sweet. Two sugars, right?"

Crystal's hippy-happy tone grated. She didn't need help, only peace. "I can do it," she snarled.

Crystal flinched and nearly spilt her tea.

Damn. Sam shot to her feet. "Sorry. I'm lousy company. Point me to a bed and I'll leave you alone, crash for an hour or two."

"Along the corridor," Knight answered, leaning against the wall, arms folded.

How long had he been standing there? She hadn't heard him return. Wondering if stuff could get any worse, she ran her fingers through her tangled hair. Her knees buckled. Knight caught her elbow before she hit the floor.

"With me." He led her away from the others and into the bedroom.

Large, like the rest of the villa, the space swamped the bed, chair, and small chest of drawers. Slivers of light slashed through the shutters and spilled onto white sheets. A fan whirred overhead.

Knight guided her to the bed and sat beside her.

"They amputated George's leg. Snake and Spanner will stay with him until he's okay to travel," he said, a slight tremor in his voice.

Straight talking, boss man. Sam's heart slammed against her ribcage, not appreciating being on the receiving end of the truth. Gripping the cuff of her shirt, she swiped a tear from the corner of her eye.

"I'll send Crystal in with your tea. Get some sleep." Knight strode out of the room.

Tears bleared the vision in her good eye. Cold bastard. The way he bossed everyone around. Dismissed her. She'd had enough of that in service. Lily might be okay with her damn alpha, but she detested the wannabe comic book superheroes. Men of few words, their arrogant tone, seldom invited questions.

When she'd first met Ed, his natural confidence had attracted her. She wanted to claim it as her own. *Not anymore.* Let Knight play the hairy hulk with someone else, and from what she remembered of Snake at the hotel, they'd cut him from the same camouflage pants. Sure, if they'd met in a bar, over a few drinks she might have invited him home, but she wanted nothing to do with the sympathy in his eyes. The way he recognised her fear. The sob lodged in her centre.

Alone, she sat on the bed in uncomfortable silence, scanning the room, for the second time in twenty-four hours, for a quick exit. Hell, she'd climb out the window if it meant she didn't have to face anyone.

A phone rang and her heart torpedoed to her toes. She leapt off the bed and rushed to the living area. Head spinning, she bit the inside of her cheek and placed a hand on the back of the sofa to steady herself. "Was that Snake? Has something happened to George?" she blurted.

"Take it easy. Like I said, the gutsy mutt is doing well," Knight answered. "We'll hook up with them tomorrow at the airport in Ouaga. Seeing as you're not ready to sleep, are you hungry? I'm pretty sure dinner is ready."

Determined not to wobble, Sam eased herself into the nearest chair. "Sure. What's on the menu?" Relieved George stood a chance of surviving, she swallowed the sour taste in her mouth and looked forward to seeing him and his grumpy owner.

CHAPTER FIVE

She'd been home from Mali for two weeks, and it felt good to be back in England.

"'Ere you are, love. Cod and chips. There are some saveloys there. On me."

"Thanks. You read my mind." Sam returned the old guy behind the counter's wink. *Hell.* He was being kind, but the thought of pig fat made her eyes roll and her stomach rolling along with the waves against the seafront wall. Mrs Inskip, the owner of the bed and breakfast, said the place rated as one of the few decent dives to eat along the seaside strip at Scarborough. Packed with locals, Sam believed her.

By the time she made it onto the street, the wind had turned bitter, blowing a gale, tossing dust and all sorts of rubbish from the narrow alley between houses, across the road, and on to the beach.

Keeping one eye on the stormy clouds rolling in from the North Sea, she picked up pace and hurried to the bed and breakfast before it poured. She tucked the packet of warm food into the front of her jacket, blew warm air into the tips of her gloves, and wrestled with her map.

Between her numb fingers and runny nose, she was having a hell of a time orientating the damn thing. The last missed turn meant she'd spent the best part of an hour walking in circles around the Scarborough lighthouse.

As usual, she'd woken up angry and left the bed and breakfast early. Snapping at strangers over burnt toast and marmalade screamed unfair and sapped her energy. There must be a path through the funk, a way to lose her rotten attitude. She'd decided to move from Oxford up North. A fresh start. Now she had to make the best of it.

The day before last, she'd yelled at Bounce. Unacceptable, all her dogs were the best. Amazing. Capable of running a rescue without her.

This break by the sea might be a corny idea, but she refused to take the damn drugs the shrink had prescribed, and it didn't sit right, leaving Baxter in charge of her animals. After all, she'd hired him the week before she went to Mali.

One evening, after a long day, she invited him and Jim to share a few beers around the fire pit. Ed had convinced her the dogs would survive while she took a few days R and R. Reluctantly she'd agreed, mainly because Jim offered to help set up the new silos while she was away. Meadow's pups were due soon, and with the extra animals to feed, the added storage capacity meant she'd save money ordering the dog kibble in larger quantities.

She hadn't known Jim much longer than Baxter, but she'd trusted the gnarly, older guy the minute he rocked up on her doorstep. Probably had a lot to do with the fact he looked a lot like her granddad. Long gone now, but she missed him every day.

Unfortunately, it didn't matter how many clifftop walks she trudged along, the wind nipping her cheeks, Bounce and the other dogs remained locked in her thoughts.

To top it off, sea air made you hungry, and thanks to her poxy sense of direction, she'd missed Miss Inskip's Devonshire tea. A three o'clock event. A sugary tourist trap she fell headlong into on her first day.

The tangy smell of salt and vinegar pricked her nostrils as she turned the corner, the strong wind chasing her the final few feet to the cottage.

She kicked the unlocked door shut behind her and hurried to her room. This morning she'd been too embarrassed to let anyone clean her mess, so she'd hung the Do Not Disturb sign on the door. Not much bigger than her bunk in the army, it shouldn't take long to straighten the shoebox single.

First things first. The sooner she demolished the fatty carbohydrates burning the shit out of her nipples, the quicker her hangover might fuck off. Since the timer on the gas heating hadn't kicked in yet, she didn't take her coat off, but undid the top buttons to slide free the greasy package. Her phone rang just as she plonked it on the bed.

"What?" Sam blasted the poor sod on the other end and kicked herself. Doomed to more bracing walks to cool her temper.

"Sam, is that you?"

"No, Lil. It's Frosty the Snowman. What can I do for you?" Her best mate didn't deserve the sarcasm, but friends could handle it. Right? "Can I call you back?" Before she attempted any meaningful conversation, she needed food, getting cold on the candlewick bedspread.

"I've been calling you for hours." Lily ignored her. Typical. A personality quirk she'd learned from being the only child of an overly indulgent, mega-rich father.

Excited and eager to give Sam the daily rundown on her daughter's day, Lily's smile carried over the phone. Usually, she looked forward to talking to her best friend about the kid. Today, not so much.

"Sorry, I'm hanging up now," she insisted before her crap mood did any more damage. "I'll call you soon, promise." She pressed the red button and tossed her phone on the bed. Abandoning the cold, soggy chips, she gathered the empty wine bottle off the carpet. After concealing it in an empty Marks and Sparks bag, she tucked it, neck down, in the wastepaper basket. *Like a dolly in a pram.* She chuckled.

In previous years, Lily had always helped her chase away Ed's ghost on his birthday. If she could stop seeing him dying, maybe she'd have a fair shot at getting on with the rest of her life. Whatever that might be.

Working with the trainee K9 handlers in Africa had been an attempt to shift her perspective, but the attack on the hotel had done the exact opposite, transporting her smack bang to Afghanistan, flooding her with shit her permanently shaky nerves did not appreciate.

Last night she'd partied alone, and one glass of cheap Chianti turned into a bottle. All day, the alcohol struggled to stay in her stomach, but it didn't keep her from swilling the dregs in the bottom of the lonely glass sitting on the bedside table. "Waste not, want not." She toasted her tired reflection in the mirror.

Desperate, much? Get a grip. She reached for her phone and rang Lily back. Usually a call with Ms Sunshine lifted her mood no matter how dark. Totally insane, considering Lily's latest bright idea.

It didn't matter how many times Sam said no, her bestie insisted on an opening party for the kennels. Lily persisted until Sam rolled over and set a date.

"Fine, Lily, but you are organising the damn thing. While you're at it, call Daddy and ask him to write a big fat cheque because I'm soddin' broke."

"I thought you'd given up swearing," Lily admonished.

"Yeah, I did. Yesterday. Today's a whole other story." She extended her arm and poked her tongue at the mobile.

"No stress, Sam. The party is my kennel-warming present. Leave it to me. I have it under control."

Mary's screech pierced Sam's ear.

"Give her to me."

Knight became a real softie around the two women in his life. It shouldn't, but it amazed her. She stifled her chuckle and waited for the kissing to stop.

"It's settled. Two weeks from this Saturday. We'll be there..." Lily's breathy sigh wafted over her phone.

"Yeah, yeah, with bells on, I know. Bye, Lily. Have fun."

"It will be perfect. Honest. Everyone will travel up for it, including Snake."

Lily's famous grin leapt from her words. "Don't you and Kate get any big ideas, Lily," she warned. Kate, especially, had earned her reputation as a mad matchmaker.

Sam shook her head, dismissing the tingly sensation in the front of her pelvis. Would it be so bad? Snake was certainly easy on the eye. "How's his dog?" She couldn't deny being curious.

"George. Breaks my heart every time I see him. Three legs, but he doesn't seem to care. He and Snake are that match made in heaven."

"Lily. Help." Knight's voice echoed in the background.

"Okay, got to rescue the nappy challenged. Talk to you soon. Love you."

"Love you, too, Lily. Soon." The click on the end of the line meant no more excuses, but even her cast-iron stomach couldn't handle cold, soggy chips. "No." She stared at the saveloy. Nothing for it, but to brave the damn weather and search for healthier food.

First, she needed to call and check on Baxter and Jim. Make sure there were no complications with the silos. After several tries, she gave up. Checking she had her room key, she headed out, wondering why no-one had answered. Then she remembered Jim grumbling about having to leave early. Something to do with a baby shower. Sam scratched her head. Made no sense to her, but Baxter would be busy finishing the job on his own. She'd try again later.

CHAPTER SIX

Frequent weather checks were a must. That had been clear from day one of her move to Giggleswick. Cold, wet, and windy with occasional snow, the norm for winter up north. and today's forecast, blazing across her laptop screen, was no different.

Not that Sam's dogs minded the wind tickling their ears, and they squinted in reverent appreciation at the first flakes of snow drifting onto their noses. A good thing because England's rain gods showered their damp hospitality on everyone anytime the mood struck.

For the life of her, she hadn't been able to figure out why Lily insisted on having an outside area for her guests to slip and slide in the mud. Not to mention, erecting the canvas marquee at an angle to the house didn't make putting the monster up any easier.

Sam steadied herself against the blustering wind roaring through the oak trees and took a sec to inhale the sweet scent of the wildflowers scattered across the moor. A reminder she had forgotten to water the potted plants. Unlike her mother, no one ever called her a green thumb.

Bounce's nose poked at the sky. "If only you spoke people, girl.

With your sense of smell, I'm sure you know the proper name for each one of these blooms. To me, they're simply pink, yellow, blue..."

Bounce's excited bark interrupted her boring list. After days of moping around, not wanting to leave the safety of the veranda, it was great to see her chirpy. Sam bit her the tip of her tongue 'til she tasted blood. The cost of holding back the sickening combination of tears and blinding anger at the way Baxter had treated her while she'd been away. Being down a hand might be a pain, but no way would Baxter set foot on her property again. She and Jim would manage.

Why had she let Lily drag her into agreeing to a party for potential customers? Not to mention her friends. Moving may not have been more impulsive than smart. It had drained her bank account, and if one of the hundred grant proposals she'd sent didn't come through, she'd have to kiss the Mates for Mates programme goodbye.

"Argh!" No matter how many times she shook the twisted thread of fairy lights, they stayed knotted. Same problem with her knitting. Another therapeutic intervention designed to take her mind off Ed, Afghanistan, the pounding of her heart. Undoing mistakes stressed more than soothed.

Lily had it in her head that the magical forest theme she saw in a dippy magazine littering the hairdressers provided the perfect vibe to attract potential investors. Sam ran her hand through the end of her long ponytail. It needed a trim—badly, including the lopsided fringe, hiding eyebrows begging for a shape.

With the canvas roof erected, at least the frozen guests might stay dry long enough for Lily to finish her speech. Grabbing a pole in one hand, a bag of nails and a hammer in the other, Sam tossed the coloured lights over the highest rung and climbed the ladder. At the top, she nudged the dangling lights to one side with her knee.

Who knew how many guests her friend had pulled together? Knowing Lily, not over the top. Enthusiastic, but shy by nature, and wary after her ex's abuse, she didn't do well in crowds.

When Knight arrived, could Sam convince him to change his wife's mind? Worth a try. If not, she'd send him into Skipton in search of portable gas heaters. She flicked the fairy light cord around her fingers and leaned over to lasso the closest pole. The ladder shook. Bracing her left knee against the edge, she balanced the hammer and nails on the top step and teased the lights along the framework of the roof. Soon she'd have the place blinking brighter than Santa's Christmas palace.

"What do you think, girl?" The German shepherd teetered on her hind legs and nudged Sam's boot, her whimper not very encouraging. "Okay, girl. Hungry, ay? Me, too. Nearly done." Wanting to finish before Tom arrived, she'd skipped lunch. She should have cancelled, but Jenna's son had plenty of upheaval in his life without her wimping on him. He regularly visited after school.

Too many things on her damn To Do List intended to plug holes where memories loved to infiltrate. A snort from below made her laugh. "Touch of hay fever, girl?" Did sarcasm even work on dogs? "A lot of help you are. Pity you can't use your front paws to hold this steady." She raised her eyes at the pole. One end lodged against her knee, the other against the ladder.

Bounce galloped rings around her, taking any conversation as a cue for play. "Not helpful, girl, unless you want me to tip arse over tit." She reached for the hammer and missed.

"I'll get it."

Even though she knew Snake would be at the party, his rich baritone rumbling behind her surprised her. She twisted to face him and caught her foot under the rung, lost her balance, and fell. Hands flailing, she found nothing to grip, but air. "Shi—"

"Whoa!" Snake's arm curled tightly around her waist, preventing her from hitting the ground. "Sorry, I didn't mean to scare you."

More startled by her reaction to his touch than him suddenly appearing out of the blue, Sam held on to his solid forearm, firm beneath the sleeve of his leather bomber jacket, a breath too long before pushing it away. "Damn it, Snake. Let go of me."

As though she'd suddenly caught fire, he did as she asked. Her arse hit the mud, damp seeping through her jeans. Served her right.

Sam slapped her wet hands together and cursed herself for being snarly. "How's your dog?" The scruffy springer spaniel sat next to him, gazing lovingly at Bounce.

"For a peg leg, he's doing fine. Aren't you boy?"

She glanced at the dog's missing back leg. "Lucky he didn't lose his head."

"Sure is. You? Aside from a wet backside, are you okay?"

As well as being deep, his voice had a lilt to it. Soothing. Laced with a genuine concern, she had no clue how to handle. "I'm fine," she muttered, digging her heels into the dirt.

"Okay, then. George. Where are your manners? Paw? That's it, boy. Say thank you to the woman who saved your life?"

She smiled at the pitiful look on the dog's face as he wobbled and raised his front paw.

Catching his alpha's approving eye, George barked, dropped his paw, and slobbered her cheek with his rough, wet tongue. *Cute.*

"Need help?" Two large hands stretched towards her.

"No. Thank you. I've got it." She hauled herself out of the mud. "Come, Bounce." In competition for the soppy eye award, traitor Bounce rolled onto her back, threw her legs in the air, and panted at George.

"Fierce protector you have there."

"Better believe it, ay girl?" Like an idiot, she paused, waiting for the dog to show support. When none came, she shifted onto her front foot and deeply regretted it. Her audible wince had Snake moving too close. Her right leg crumpled underneath her. Strong hands clasped her hips to steady her.

Grow up. She smiled because the way his gaze scanned her boobs steamed with adult vibes. His fresh pine woodsy smell screamed male.

Sam didn't need to see him naked to know every inch of him had to be gorgeous. The type of man she used to have no problem seducing. Fighting not to stare at his chiselled feature, the full lips, she shifted her gaze to the trees over his shoulder. She needed to get laid.

Realising she probably smelled of all things manure, she ducked her head, released the death grip she had on his forearm, and wiped her sweaty palm on her pants.

Snake huffed. "It's been a long drive." His lips quirked into a lopsided grin. The chipped front tooth added to his boyish look. A look that contradicted the rest of him. "I could do with a shower, but I'm not contagious. Promise."

Yes, well, she couldn't be entirely sure about the catching bit. "You're early. Where are your partners in crime? I thought Lily said you were driving up together."

"We did, but I brought my vehicle. They carried on into town to fetch the booze. I've brought the food. Lots of food. I hear you're baking the cake."

"Not me. Hopefully, Spanner's got that covered. I'm responsible for the fairy grotto." She swept her hand in front of the half-erected marquee. Snake raised an eyebrow, and she couldn't hold back her smile.

"Yes, well, it's not finished. By the way, there's not much room in the house. The couples have taken up all the spare beds. I've set up the bunk over the barn for you."

"Sounds great, but I don't want to put you to any trouble. Want me to find a room in town?"

"Fat chance. Anyway, it's no trouble. I might pitch a tent outside myself. Follow me. I'll give you a quick tour, and then you're on your own. I have stuff to do this afternoon. Make yourself at home. Not sure where you parked, but there's room up by the barn. Get settled while you wait for the others to arrive. There's beer and a shepherd's pie in the house." Her stomach growled.

"Thanks." Snake nodded at the foot she couldn't put weight on and grinned. "Where's the nearest chair?"

Smug git. She turned to lead him up to the barn but didn't get far before her ankle gave way.

Sam's fingers curled around his arm. Her full lips rolled together, straining not to smile. Pity. He'd lay down a month's pay that behind her frown she hid a brilliant smile, but right now, she wasn't sharing the love with him, which made him fucking jealous of those she honoured.

She had to be a foot shorter than him, and until a few seconds ago, she hadn't taken her eyes off him. The strain on her neck must be killing her. Not that he minded looking at her face. Pretty didn't describe it, and those eyes were something else. Brown, but the shade changed depending on the light from rich dark chocolate to amber.

"Steady." One hand lightly holding her elbow, the other hovering over her lower back, he walked with her to a wicker chair on the wooden veranda. Bounce settled beside her and placed a paw on her knee, George hot on her tail.

"Point me to that fridge, and I'll fetch you some ice for your ankle."

"Okay, thanks. Through there. There's a clean tea towel in the drawer by the sink. Grab a couple of beers while you're there."

The way Sam rubbed her ankle said it hurt a lot more than she cared to admit. "Sure. Here, put your leg on this." Snake reached for a stool and placed it under her lower leg. "I'll be right back. George, heel."

"Sorry, there's a no dog in the house rule."

"No problem. George, stay." The dog shuffled next to Bounce and rested his two front paws on Sam's big toe. No risk of her moving anywhere. As he opened the screen door, she pulled her phone from her pocket.

"Hi, Tom. Sorry, something has come up. I'll have to cancel today. See you tomorrow."

Who the hell was Tom? A boyfriend? Wouldn't surprise him. A stunning-looking woman. A single bat of Sam's eyelids, the sway of her sweet arse. *Shit*, any man would be a fool not to come running.

CHAPTER SEVEN

Sam took her hand off the wall, stared at the mirror on the back of her bedroom door, rolled her shoulders, and fixed her face in a well-practiced, nothing hurting here grin. Sleep hadn't been the cure she'd hoped for. Ever since Lily and the gang arrived, they had fussed worse than the bees in her hives.

Last night, she'd given up objecting, let Knight light the fire, bit back her comments, and allowed them to debate whether she'd broken her ankle. There were growls all round when she flatly refused to go to the hospital. She expected it from the Sentinel alphas, but when Lily joined in, she politely told everyone where to go and hobbled to bed.

When she woke up, the pain in her ankle hadn't gone away. She swore under her breath, showered, and dressed. *Come on, bubble-gut. You can do this.* Fixing a smile on her face, she opened the door and limped into the living area.

She got as far as the back of the sofa and Snake shoved a makeshift walking stick at her hand. "Here, take this."

"I hope you weren't awake the entire night making this. Reluctant to admit she needed the aid, she waved the stick away. "You'd make an excellent nurse. Thank God Doc hasn't arrived yet. One medic on site is plenty."

"Hey, don't knock it. Some of my best friends are nurses." He winked at Kate, who shook her head.

"Mine too, and to prove it, let me buy you a hat. One of those with the big red cross," Sam offered, but when Snake's expression changed subtly, hurt mixed with frustration, she guessed he didn't like being teased. "Blimey, Mr Sensitive. Okay. Hand me the damn stick. I can push the crowd out of the way."

This morning they'd planned a shopping trip for the girls in Skipton, the market town, about a half-hour drive from the kennels. But the Yorkshire Dales offered no competition for London's West End. At least Lily let her finish her coffee before she tugged on her arm.

"Let's go, Sam. Crys left a half-hour ago. Kate, are you sure you won't come?"

"No, I'll hang out and wait for Doc," she replied with a grin.

Sam resisted an eye roll. The way these intelligent, independent women missed their men always struck her as embarrassing.

"You sure your ankle will hold up?" Snake asked.

Again, with the worry in his sunny blue eyes. Odd, disconcerting, the way his concern made her heart flutter. Maybe she should stay, supervise the list of jobs she'd given him last night. Rug up on the veranda, a mug of cocoa in hand, and ogle Snake's toned muscles flexing and straining while he hefted hay.

Sam sighed. "Stop fussing, Snake. My ankle will cope. Kate did an excellent taping job, and I can always grab Lily's arm, right?"

"No problem." Lily linked arms and patted her hand, humming *Lean On Me* as she grinned them both to the door.

"Bye, Snake. Hope I didn't leave you too much hard work? You asked, remember?"

"No problem. Happy to take on whatever you dish out." His eyes sparkled. "I feel responsible for you taking the tumble," he added.

Now that was sweet of the six-foot-plus giant, but she threw in the snort. "Get over it, hunk. I stupidly climbed the ladder with no free hand."

Lily reckoned the man's computer skills were off the chart, so he'd have no trouble making a fortune in the civilian world. If Snake had a safe job, instead of being Sentinel's comms man, Sam might have explored the ping of lust zinging in her pelvis, their physical attraction, but she didn't date men who enjoyed hunting the adrenaline rush.

"Lily, let's go. Bounce. Stay." Her dog got on well with George and it hadn't escaped her how the pair mirrored their mutual attraction. *Except Bounce shows a damn sight more grace.*

Unable to let Snake get away entirely with his earlier flirty comment, she blew him a kiss and stumbled after Lily. "Slow down." She pointed at the veranda steps.

Determined not to look back as they drove away, Sam sat with her hands curled in her lap, sniffed in a long breath, and tried to forget her throbbing ankle. But, last minute, as they rounded the bend at the bottom of the driveway, she turned.

Snake didn't disappoint. Flagged by George and Bounce, he leaned against the front door, all long legs and tough guy chest, returning her kiss. Even from this distance, the sparkle in his eyes pierced her heart.

Shi… Shivers. This has to stop. With a smile lifting her cheeks, she ducked behind her seat. When had she become stingy about sharing pleasure? *The day Ed died.* Her reserve had nothing to do with Snake, and everything to do with her no-military-men-as-fuck-buddy policy.

"We have to stop at the florists on the way home and pick up the flowers." Lily ripped through her thoughts, her excitement a notch above acceptable decibel level for this early in the morning.

"Flowers? Sodding 'ell, Lil. I'm not getting married."

"Oh, stop being such a grouch. Your place needs cheering up."

"Thanks," she humphed. There'd been no time for nesting, as Lily called it. Other than moving furniture into the house, she hadn't wasted time tizzying the place. "I must admit, Lily, I'm impressed. Who knew Giggleswick had a florist?"

"More importantly than flowers, you better hope we bought plenty of champagne. It's not as though we can nick out to the local off-licence."

Sam collapsed against her friend, giggling, something she hadn't done in a long time. "You crack me up. We have more booze than the bloody off-licence."

"Yes, well, we can talk about that later. We're here." Country life had its pluses. Skipton wasn't small, but unlike London, they didn't have to search for miles looking for a place to park. Lily pulled up across the street from the dress shop. "Time to put your game face on and think glam."

They were crossing the country road when, out of nowhere, a car headed straight for them. Sam half-turned in time to see Lily throw herself forward out of range of a direct hit and sprang after her. Her ankle buckled, sending her flying onto the concrete. Arse for feet was wearing very thin. The car wheels screeched as it sped around the corner and out of sight.

"You okay?" Lily asked, kneeling beside her.

"Yeah, I'm fine." She winced and raised two fingers at the prick tearing up the country road. "Peace, muppet."

"What the hell? He drove straight for you." Lily pulled her phone from her pocket. "I'm calling Daniel."

"No. Don't call Knight or we'll never hear the end of it." The car had moved too fast for her to get a clear view of the number plate, but she'd bet Baxter was the driver. All this party stuff made her paranoid. Even sleepy Skipton must have their share of hoon drivers.

"What about your ankle? If you don't want me to call Daniel, I'll call Crys."

"God no. I swear if I leave now, it's over. You will never get me back here," she said with a chuckle.

"Okay, but I'm not happy."

"Yeah, yeah, mum. Don't be such a drama queen and help me up. Give me your hand."

"What do you think?"

The dressing room curtain screeched on the overhanging rail. "What the feck, Lily?" Sam clutched the crumpled flag of material pretending to be a dress to her chest. As soon as she'd stripped to her undies and faced up to trying the damn dress on, she should have chosen a cubicle that had a door with a lock. "A bit of privacy while a girl shuffles her lumps." Or in her case, bumps. Her chest pimples seldom made a man's eyes pop.

"Shy, Sam? You are joking? That colour suits you." Lily grabbed the top of her dress before Sam screamed stop.

"The colour is not my problem. Freezing my tits off, on the other hand..." Sam tossed the dress on the bench and snatched a pair of black silk pants off the hook.

"Oh, no, you don't. You promised. If you had your way, you'd arrive at your party in jeans and an anorak. Try this one on." Lily held up a dress made from material destined for a life in an out of the dry cleaners.

"No." The pink fluff covered in beads was worse than the striped number, and since when had this become her party?

"I thought we got past this when we were college roomies. You have the best legs. They're that long. I swear they hook onto your shoulder blades. Think again if you believe I will let you hide them in a pair of pants. Not even if they are silk." Lily snatched the pants from her hands. "We are not walking out of here until you have a dress paid for and dangling off your arm in a designer bag."

"Wow, Lil. You are cute when you stamp your foot, but my vote's a hard negative. It's not the bloody BAFTAs. The glitz can keep. Silk top and pants are as classy as it gets for the opening of dog kennels."

"Rubbish! The kennel opening is Giggleswick's..." Lily's eyes crossed. "Social event of the year." One hand braced against the wall, Lily cracked up at the daft name for the village.

Sam joined her. Giggleswick. No one said the word without cracking a smile. More appropriate for a make-believe spot in a kid's book. A perfect place. A place to move on with life. Nothing depraved happened in a place named Giggleswick.

Lily enjoyed rescuing people. Feeling broken and battered after leaving the service, Lily's kind heart and sense of fun had kept Sam from tossing herself off London Bridge. They'd been roommates in college. A no judgement haven. Dirty clothes slung over the arm of a sofa, or a chair, were the norm, and no one apologised for leaving dirty dishes in the sink.

Most afternoons, after lectures, Lily made tea. They shared a packet of digestives, licking off the chocolate, before they dunked it in their tea. Sam refused to imagine life without her best friend. Something she had in common with Knight.

Lily shoved her hand in her mouth and bit her knuckles. "Don't laugh when their royal highnesses, Will and Kate, front up at your opening. Better practise your courtesy."

Sam shook her head, waiting for a friend to get over herself. "You are nuts. Living proof motherhood robs you of a brain."

Lily punched her shoulder. "Less of that. You love Mary. Now tell me, what do you think of this creation?" She twirled in front of her.

"The dress is gorgeous. You are gorgeous." Without trying, Lily turned thrift shop clobber into designer creations. "You will drive Knight out of his superhero mind." The deep blue of the silk sculpted Lily's perfect figure and brought out the colour in her eyes. Not that her husband would look at her face—not for long, anyway.

"That's the plan." Her eyebrows hitched. Love suited her, and as for their daughter, Mary? A sweetheart who had her parents tightly wound around her pudgy finger.

Breath caught in Sam's throat. Being a mum didn't figure in her future, but she loved kids. Wished things might be different, but no kid deserved damaged goods for a mother. She undid the zip on the second dress and slipped it over her head.

"Oh my god, Sam. Why didn't you say? The bruises from your fall are already showing."

Once a nurse, always a nurse, Lily poked the one on her stomach. "Hey, hands to yourself. It's nothing. I bruise easily." She rolled her lips together and wiggled her arms into the sleeves.

"Those evil black blotches are more than nothing. I bet they hurt."

"No worse than the ones I got from an argument I had with a couple of hay bales last week."

If she'd guessed Baxter might get physical when she let him go, she might have been better prepared. He'd pushed her hard into the wall, but she had landed a few mean ones to his ribs before she ploughed her left hook into his face.

Surrounded by hangers and piles of discarded try-ons, Lily rolled her eyes.

Sam chuckled. "Jeez, Lil, you look more like Knight every day."

"I do not."

They fell against one another, cackling loudly.

"Do," Sam insisted.

Lily pinched the top of her arm. "Come on, there's a pub on the way home. Let's find Crystal and adjourn. I'll buy us lunch, and you can tell me what's going on with you and Snake."

"What? Now you're hallucinating. There is nothing to tell, but my tongue is hanging out for a beer. Anything to end this girly torture. You can drive."

Lily winked. "Get dressed. I'll meet you at the register in five minutes. Where *we* will pay for our dresses."

The curtain tinkled closed. Sam caught her reflection in the mirror. The pink silk swayed an inch below her knees. Her once-a-year day when she wore a dress. Except for her feet, she didn't look half-bad. The half-laced boots were a touch over the top, but they supported her ankle, which she needed to ice before she tracked down the twat who tried to run them over earlier.

CHAPTER EIGHT

Sam spat on her fingertips, gingerly testing the heat of the iron. Having her dress go up in flames was the last thing she wanted.

She loathed ironing. As a teenager, Sam never understood why every Wednesday evening her mother took pride in pounding knife-edge creases into everything from socks to sheets. But she had played her part and, every week, collected the laundry on her way home from school.

One afternoon, she had struggled home with the load, eager to share the news she had won a prize. Shocked not to find her mother at the ironing board, she'd eventually tracked her to a chair in the kitchen, staring out of the window. The reason never clear, not even after all these years, but everything changed that day.

"Mum, I won!" She'd wriggled the silver trophy, trying to catch her mother's glazed eyes.

"Yes, dear. Stop waving the thing in front of my face." Her nose twitched as though the prize smelt unpleasant. "It's very nice. Small."

"It's more than a cup, mum. There's a scholarship. Money won't be a problem when I go to college."

Her mother's eyes narrowed.

Sam recognised the resistance, figured it had a lot to do with being a single mother whose dreams never ventured beyond a tub full of nappies. Her father had died in a car accident rushing to the hospital. Her being born ruined more than one life.

The iron hissed, demanding more water. "Don't keep on, Samantha. I said, it's nice, but I don't understand why you want to go to college. You have everything you need here. I'm sure our local vet will take you on if you insist on working with animals." Her mother's gaze vaulted to the more fascinating events plodding by the window.

"Now put the damn thing away. The iron is waiting."

The words hammered her brain. Ironing, a life sentence, meant to shackle her to the home, in four simple words, passed to her. As soon as she left high school, she rebelled over many things, joined the army, and signed up for the K9 unit. Her way of paying for college.

She'd vowed never to iron, ever again. Except, here she was adjusting the dial, cursing Lily, and praying she didn't singe the paper-thin fabric. Lily's guests had arrived hours ago. The fact Sam didn't know half of them offered the perfect excuse to hide out in the laundry for as long as possible.

Bounce sniffed and whined, nudging Sam's thigh with her paw. "Okay, girl, good enough, ay? Give me a sec to slide into this madness, and we can have a drink." She flipped the warm dress over her head and fumbled with the tiny zipper.

Footsteps slapped the slate floor outside the laundry. Too heavy for Lily. Half expecting Knight's bossy face, she offered a salute to whoever poked their head around the door. Snake's cocky grin surprised her. An audible gasp escaped her lips as his long legs strode the last few steps to her.

"There you are. Lily reckons you're hiding. She sent me to fetch you."

His sexy baritone rumbled in his chest, warming her body, neck to toe. "No, not hiding. I'm on a mission to fix this dress." Snake's gaze did a second pass over her torso. A little uneasy, she spun in a nervous twirl.

"And?" he asked, cocking his head to one side. George, his shadow, mirrored the gesture.

"And what?" Sam shifted to her left, trying to dodge the intensity of his blue eyes. Almost opaque in the bright light.

"Mission accomplished?"

"Er, yes. Roger that. Do I pass muster?"

"Ma'am, yes ma'am. Love the boots." He winked. "How's the ankle holding up?" His gaze travelled from her feet to her non-existent cleavage.

To hell with the suggestive crap, the flirting. She leaned a fraction closer to him and sniffed deeply, searching for his woodsy scent. It must be the dress giving her courage. Her insides tingled. *Kiss me.* Yep, had to be the dress. Pink fluff in search of Cinderella's prince.

"My ankle's fine, handsome. Let's do this party before I run for the hills."

"Handsome?" Snake chuckled.

For sure, a man as fuck-me gorgeous as him was no stranger to compliments. "Yeah, don't be coy and don't get any big ideas. I'm being polite."

"Fine, but don't be gentle on my account. I can take it rough."

Bloody hell. Her lungs tightened as every atom of oxygen left the room. She didn't mind a bit of rough, either. Might be worth the risk if he wanted one night. Sexual relief from the stress of having a crowd floating around her home.

Showing outstanding self-restraint, she ignored the invitation in his cheeky smile and tipped her chin at Bounce. "Come."

"Yes, ma'am." Snake clicked his heels.

With a smile, she crooked her finger at the hounds following her out of the laundry.

Fuck me dead. Snake meant that from the tip of his horny head to his titillated toes. What did Sam weigh? One hundred and ten pounds in her boots? The backpack he trekked up and down mountains weighed more.

"You forgot to change your shoes," he murmured, surprised any words made it from his mouth given the blood had hightailed it from his brain the moment he set eyes on her in all that pink.

"I didn't forget." She spun to face him, and the twist to her ankle cost her.

"Right." He side-stepped Bounce and caught Sam's elbow.

"Thanks."

"No problem." Earlier, he'd noticed her limping and couldn't figure out why she wouldn't let him help. Her ankle needed medical attention, an x-ray, to make sure there were no broken bones.

Snake's gaze wandered over her entire body, once, twice. When she shook free from his grip and kept heading for the party, he levelled with her shoulder, ready to catch her the next time she stumbled. *Damn, woman.* Like a true bastard, he wavered between admiring the way Sam's nipples hardened and pebbled under the scrap of material doing its best to act as a dress and wanting to tear off his jacket and sling it round her shoulders.

As she didn't shiver or complain, he gave into lust and tossed the eyeballs in for round three. Who said women were the weaker sex? A few moments ago, he could have sworn she'd almost made the move and kissed him. A woman in control. Not his usual preference, but his cock jerked, keen for her to try.

His fingers took a light hold of her wrist before Spanner lobbed in front of them, faking a bow.

"Hey, it's the lady of the hour. May I have the honour of this dance, Sam?"

Knob'ed had obviously had one or two. Not drunk, but guys of their height needed to have tight control of their long limbs or they'd become unintended flying missiles. Snake tightened his grip on

Sam's wrist, which earned him a "hey," before she stepped away from him.

"Thanks, Spanner, I'd love to, but my ankle is a little…"

"No problem, milady." Spanner circled Sam's waist with one arm and pulled her off her feet, knocking several chairs over as he twirled her in a circle.

Snake saw red on fucking red. If Spanner didn't take his hands off Sam right now, he would deck the fool.

Sam shot daggers his way and growled. *Erotic as hell.* Didn't matter, it had the desired effect. He backed away. Her own woman. If she wanted to end up in a wheelchair, he had no business arguing.

Supported in Spanner's arms, her mind let go, worked itself free under the marquee, with every spin around the tiny dance floor. The heat of his body warmed her chilled bones but didn't set her on fire. Not like the way it might have if Snake had swept her off her feet.

Numb with cold, her fingers lost their grip on Spanner's neck. A broad grin swept across his face and he set her on her feet, but didn't let go of her waist. She'd never known Spanner to drink too much. None of the Sentinel men did. Her discomfort must have been noticeable because, without warning, Snake and Crystal arrived, each grabbing one of Spanner's arms.

"Er. Thanks for the dance, Spanner." Surprised and more than a little embarrassed, she didn't know what else to say.

Crystal sighed. "No problem. Twinkle Toes can't resist twirling beautiful women around the dance floor. Right, hun?"

Spanner shrugged and gently pried Crystal's fingers from his arm. "You know me, hun."

Sam frowned. They'd only met a few times, but she sure as heck didn't think Crystal would put up with an arse and she'd rather not be in the middle of whatever was going on between them. "Sorry, I need…"

"A seat." Snake took full control of her arm and led her to the nearest table.

"Catch you later, Sam," Spanner slurred and laid his chin on top of Crystal's head.

"Come on, hun. You need coffee, lots of coffee. Sam, you okay?" Crystal asked.

Sam nodded and closed her eyes, trying to make sense of the last very weird five minutes.

"Sit. Take a load off that ankle. Tea, diet coke, or something stronger?" Snake asked, turned, and headed for the house.

What the hell was wrong with Sentinel men? Tears she had no intention of allowing any further than her eyelashes rose without warning and pricked her eyeballs. Inappropriate, but her emotions were all over the place lately, overwhelmed by stuff she usually shrugged off. Her chest tightened, and it felt as though she might suffocate. She needed air, fast. Sam slipped out of the tent. A bloody bunny rabbit on the run, except there were no scary headlights.

CHAPTER NINE

Hard to tell whether Snake's simple question or the delicious hitch of his right eyebrow had sent her running for the outside loo. The wooden box, a remnant of the original farmhouse, it hadn't been used in years. Small and dark, if it wasn't for the manky smell, it could have been a perfect spot to bawl her eyes out and pull herself together.

Perched on the loo, far from being claustrophobic, the tiny space calmed her racing heartbeat. Slivers of light bleeding through several broken slats shed ample light to see her toes. Her ankle throbbed.

Sam doubted Snake had followed her, but in case he did, she braced the sole of her bare foot flat against the door. A cramp snatched at her calf. Breath lodged like a stuck fishbone in her throat. *Suck it up, Princess.*

How come Snake had such an effect on her? Ed never stirred her blood that way, and she'd considered marrying him. She loathed being attracted to the giant protector, but more than his perfect looks caught her breath. Snake had a way of smiling at people, a genuine appreciation of others twinkling in his eyes.

Lying in bed last night, listening to the wind roll over the moor, she wondered if they'd met before her military service, whether he might have asked her on a date. She flicked a moth off the wall. If she hadn't insisted on going to see Arash that day. *Don't go there.* But she had and, unlike Ed, she had lived. Simple stuff like a caring man concerned over her dumb ankle, asking if she wanted a drink, sent her running. Unable to face what? Kindness. Moments she didn't deserve—moments she had no right to hope might last.

Sam cradled her cheeks in her palms and shook her head. "You're having a bad day. You've had them before. They pass." Saying it out loud helped. Words swinging off cobwebs hanging from the door filled the emptiness inside and out. Conversations with inanimate objects or Bounce were the best company when your world imploded and left you alone—small.

"Sam?"

Feck. Did it really surprise her Snake had followed? He'd been stuck to her side at the party, sensing her uneasiness. Gripping every muscle, she willed him to go away. Another cramp seized her calf and then her toes curled into a grotesque fist at the end of her leg.

The space between the loo and the other side of the door pulsed with silence. A wordless drone, set to pounce, but hell would freeze over before she answered him. Seconds later, a door slammed. *Yes.* Relieved Snake had given up and returned to the party, she relented and let her tears fall. Once the emotion flowed, the episode, according to her shrink, should end soon. She dabbed her eyes and sniffed.

"Was it something I said?" Snake asked.

His deep voice was catnip for her anxiety. She glanced up at the rugged face peering over the top of the door. Good job her knickers weren't dancing around her ankles. His grin sent tingles spinning around the walls of her stomach. "Go away."

"No can do. Not until I know you're okay."

"Oh, for Pete's sake." She kicked open the door.

Snake leaned against the outside wall, arms crossed, a blade of wet grass between his teeth. Bounce and George lay side by side next to him, looking far too frigging comfortable. He scanned her body and grunted. As usual, she felt naked and bloody freezing, but that didn't stop her pelvis from zinging with possibilities. "What the fu...?"

"... flying fairy?" the idiot offered, flashing his annoying, uncannily perfect, imperfect smile.

"I'd have said fuck, but have it your way." A sniff strangled her next sentence, but he got the message. Unwanted attendance.

"'Scuse me if I'm a tad concerned. My mistake, but you turned sheet white when I offered you a diet coke. Hightailed it out of the kitchen as though I pulled the pin on a live grenade." He turned to leave, whistling for the dogs to follow.

"No. Sorry. I just needed air." Which sounded bizarre, seeing as they'd been in a tent, and why did she have to speak—give him grounds to stay?

"Here." He handed her a grubby piece of cloth.

"Big on hankies?"

"Nah. Must have picked it up this morning when I helped Knight change Mary's, er... nappy." He grinned.

"Yeah, well, keep it. I don't need it."

"Whatever you say. It's a tad chilly to be sitting out here." He nodded at her bare foot. "Want to grab my arm and go inside where it's warm? Promise I won't ask any more tough questions."

"Hilarious. No, I think I'll sit here for a bit, and I'm not looking for company. Thanks for coming to check, but don't let me keep you from enjoying the party."

"Okay." He half-turned. "Is the ankle bothering you?"

Before she answered, he squatted in front of her. Military men moved fast, part of their training, but Snake's speed bordered on the preternatural.

His large hand covered her knee. A featherweight touch that instantly slowed her hammering heart. She'd never accuse Snake of being insensitive, not if she wanted to be fair. "Persistent, aren't you?"

He shrugged. Strong, silent insistence his thing, with the bonus of a smile. She should hire him as a trainer. "George has gone." Sam nodded at the paddock as if it were an invitation for him to follow.

"Uh huh. Off to more important stuff. Bounce likes to share her stash of party bones." His heels shuffled in the dirt. It had to be uncomfortable, squatting, trying to keep their knees from touching.

Sam sneezed, took the rag when he offered it again. "Figures. She's taken to your three-legged cowboy."

"Want to talk about it?"

"Bone sharing? Not particularly. Thanks again. I'll catch up with you later." She tried to stand, but with zero manoeuvring space, she stumbled. *Shit.* She needed air. More air.

Snake ached to help Sam, but she didn't have to tell him twice. Hell, he'd lost count of how many times she'd given him the brush-off. A man could take a hint. If she wanted to play martyr, have at it. He'd check on her later, in case her stubborn arse collapsed under a tree or fell down a well.

He dug in his heel and turned just as a shadow crossed his path. Someone else shared his interest in Sam's outside bog.

"Baxter, what the hell do you want?" Sam snarled.

Snake smiled, taking comfort in the fact she didn't reserve her snarly self solely for him. Maintaining eye contact with the intruder, he took in the man's height, a tad shorter but over six feet. Hair cut military short.

"Oh, now that hurts, love. Why didn't you invite me to your party?"

"Fuck off."

That's the Sam we know and love. No mistake. *Persona non grata.* Instinctively, Snake shifted in front of her, curled his hands into fists and blocked Baxter's direct access. He should have expected Sam's next move. A sharp elbow dig to his ribs, and she slipped around him to face off with the stranger. Champion effort, given her chin strained to reach the guy's chest.

Every muscle in his body drew to attention, prepared to step in if the guy so much as flinched. "Hey, mate, why don't you—"

"Thanks, Snake, I can handle this." Sam moved in front of him, once more taking point. "Baxter, I told you the other day. You aren't welcome here." Sam cocked her head in his direction. A two-for-one statement. "If you've come to collect your belongings, they're not here. I left them with Linda at the post office this morning. You can pick it up there."

"I got it. But there's stuff missing."

"Yeah. Like what?"

"My toolbox. I'm not looking for trouble. I'll go on over to my bunk, find it, and be on my way. Maybe grab a beer and say hello to your friends."

"There was no box. And it's a negative on the beer."

"Oh yeah. You owe me."

Baxter stepped forward, towering over Sam. *Too close, fucker.* Snake waved a finger.

"Stand down, Snake. I can handle this," Sam said.

Snake didn't take his eyes off Baxter, his invitation clear. *One more step, dickhead, and you're mine.*

"Tomorrow, when I pay you this week's wages, I'll put an extra week in your account to compensate for anything you think you've lost. Now get off my property before I let the dogs loose." She rolled her eyes at Snake.

Now you're talking.

"Generous, but nothing more than I'm owed, and I still want what's mine." Baxter raised his fist.

Quicker than he expected, Sam dodged the man's right hook, but speed cost her on her injured ankle. Off balance, the bastard clipped her chin with his return swing.

Snake roared and lunged. Two seconds later, he had Baxter's wrist twisted between his shoulder blades, ready to smash his head into the wall.

"Stop. Let him go," Sam said.

"No way. What the fuck, arsehole?" He grabbed the other wrist. "I should break both your arms. A reminder never to lay your hand on another woman."

"Snake, please. Leave it."

Sam's thin voice tore through the blackness tormenting the edges of Snake's vision. He loosened his grip on the man's arm. Baxter spat and took off along the path.

"This isn't the end, love. I'll be back for my property. Count on it," he yelled over his shoulder.

Snake hesitated, torn between going after him and taking care of Sam. Her face had turned as white as the snow on the top of the fence post. Her hands hung rigid by her sides and her breaths came short and heavy through her nose. "You okay?"

"Fine. It's nothing."

"Again with the nothings. Seems to me your nothings equate to anyone else's hell of a something. I don't get why you're letting this arsehole walk away, but I'm not arguing. I'm on your side. Forget the diet coke. My guess is you could do with something stronger."

He took her elbow and pulled her closer. If she wanted to wobble away from him, his grip was light. A sharp tug and she'd be free. Her eyes rolled to the sky and looked as though she was about to faint. "Whoa there." Fucking arsehole must have hit her harder than he realised. Scooping her into his arms, Snake caught her before she hit the ground and carried her into the house.

The others had abandoned the marquee and were kicking back under the shelter of the front veranda. Knowing Sam didn't appreciate being the centre of attention, he detoured around the side to the back stairs. Upstairs, there were only a few rooms, so her bedroom didn't take long to find. A large bed dominated the small space.

Aside from a bedside table and a few photos on the wall, it was empty.

Concerned Sam hadn't opened her eyes, he laid her carefully in the centre of the bed, took hold of her slim wrist, and checked her pulse.

CHAPTER TEN

Anger coursed through Snake's veins, feeding his desire to tear that fucker Baxter apart. Make sure he never so much as looked cross-eyed at any woman again.

Sam's pulse beat strong under his fingers, and she had no trouble breathing, but she'd taken a powerful blow to her chin. Her lip had swollen, and a bruise had started to show. It could be a while before she came round. What had Baxter meant? Snake might not know Sam well, but she'd never hold onto property that didn't belong to her.

She moaned and shivered. Fridges were warmer than Sam's bedroom and she'd be much more comfortable in the bed, not on top of it, but he couldn't see any sleepwear and didn't trust himself to undress her. The folds of the flimsy dress clinging to the soft curves of her slim frame, the smooth lines undulating beneath silk, impossible to achieve wearing underwear, set Snake's blood on fire.

She moaned again as he reached for the duvet and pulled it over her slim shoulders. Made sure he tucked the edges around her body. His hand moved slowly, seeking permission to show her his touch could bring pleasure, take away her pain. Heart pounding, he willed the snow sticking to the skylight above him to fall harder and cool the heat blazing through his overactive libido.

Watching Sam earlier, stubbornly insisting on dancing with Spanner, his cock had taken notice of how, despite her painful ankle, her delicate bones had swayed sensuously to the music. Not even her fondness for working boots detracted from her natural grace. *Shit, keep it in check.* Next thing, he'd be writing bloody poetry.

Harder than he'd been for any woman in a long time, he'd resisted cutting in, nursed another beer, and thanked God her eyes were closed, and she couldn't see him lusting after her. Sam took his breath away.

He enjoyed her sense of play. The tease. His heart had missed a beat, imagining her slender limbs coiled around his waist as he pounded into her.

Fixing his gaze on the gentle rise and fall of her chest, he shifted to the chair beside the bed. What made this beauty tick? Bewitched, he wanted to understand everything. The highs, every low.

Sam stirred, frowning deeply, murmuring incoherently. He grabbed the extra blanket from the foot of the bed.

"What happened?" She tried to sit.

"Steady, you took one on the chin and blacked out. Here, drink this." He reached for the glass of water beside the bed and cupped the back of her head. "Take your time." He pressed the glass to her lips. "Want to tell me what's going on?"

"There isn't anything to tell. Sorry, I'm behaving like a right Nellie. If it wasn't for this stupid ankle, I'd..." Her toes wiggled under the mound of blankets. "Baxter, the twat, would be the one limping away."

"No doubt in my mind. You've got quite a swing, slugger. Remind me not to get any closer to your bad side. What's dickhead's problem?"

"I fired him."

"Why?" None of his business, but one thing she should be sure of, no one would ever lay a finger on her again. Not in anger.

"He used to work here. I hired him to help with odd jobs, but I didn't appreciate the way he treated my dogs. A couple of weeks ago, I left him and another employee, Jim, working on installing the new silos while I stupidly went away for a few days. He promised to take care of the dogs.

"I returned early, unexpected, and caught him beating Meadow, my pregnant shepherd, and then I saw Bounce chained to the rail outside the barn. The son of a bitch had placed her feed bowl outside the reach of the chain. When I saw blood on her neck, I lost it."

His gut somersaulted. Damn certain he couldn't handle seeing Sam cry, he grabbed the hand closest to him before his head objected, brought it to his lips, and blew on her fingertips. "Easy, tiger. Take another sip." With his free hand, he offered her the water. Sam shivered. "Get under the covers. I'll get some ice for your jaw." Snake lowered the glass before any water spilt and nodded at the empty grate. "Best start the fire, too. Snow is setting in for the night."

"Thanks."

Her lips started to curl, and he hoped she might smile. His heart howled when she didn't.

"Give me a couple of hours and I'll chop more wood," she said.

"Sure." With a gentle push, he encouraged her shoulders into the pillows. "A punch to the face hurts." He'd certainly experienced a few blows over the years. "Don't pretend it doesn't. Rest. Doc should check you out, make sure you don't have a concussion."

The next second Sam had his wrist in a death grip trying to haul herself forward. "Forget that. What we should do is get our arses back to the party. Trust me, you think Knight has a temper? It's nothing compared to Lily's revenge if we miss her bloody gala affair."

They should bottle Sam's determination. She looked as though she'd gone ten rounds with Godzilla. Not that his cock cared. *Hell. Get a grip.* "We could, but last time I checked, I doubt they've noticed we're missing. Humour me and grab those couple of hours.

Tomorrow I'll be gone, and things will be back to normal. You and your furry friends can knock yourselves out. For now, rest. I'll square it with Lily, tell her you had to take care of the dogs. Then I'll chop the wood."

He worked hard at keeping the edge from his voice. It pissed him off the way she insisted on not needing help. Sentinel's sole purpose was protector stuff. The need to help those who couldn't take of themselves ran in his blood. "Could you eat something?"

Sam winced.

"Sorry, dumb question. Maybe some ice cream? Or do you want to sleep?"

"Sleep. Thanks. Sorry, Snake, before, I didn't mean to snap, but I'm not used to company. I don't get many visitors. Hard to believe your parents named you after a reptile. What's your real name?"

And best he left it right there before he offered to stay until he made sure Baxter no longer posed a threat. "Sleep, it is. Good call. You'll feel better in the morning. The name's John. Nothing flash."

"Suits you. John. I appreciate you…" Sam waved her hand in the air. "Taking care of stuff."

No one had called him by his first name since he was a kid, and he couldn't imagine it becoming a habit, but his name hanging on Sam's breath? He could get used to it. "Don't worry. I'll take care of the dogs, and then come and keep watch." He tapped his head. "Concussion watch." He ignored her humph. "Where do you keep their food?"

"Out by the water tanks. We had to move the silos again. Don't ask. There's a feeding schedule pinned to the wall." Exhausted, her head sank into the pillow and her eyes drifted shut.

Snake stroked the hair from her forehead with the edge of his thumb. After he lit the damn fire and spoke to the others, he should pack, get an early start for London. Kate or Crystal could watch Sam. She should be fine by morning.

"John." Sam sighed.

He leaned closer, his lips hovering against her ear. "Yes."

"It's cold."

"Fire coming up. Sleep."

CHAPTER ELEVEN

Over thirty and Sam firmly believed monsters lived under the bed or lurked behind the curtain, planning her violent death, willing her to stay asleep so they could chop her into little bits and shove her bloodied remains in the basement freezer.

No different tonight. Every hour, she cracked opened at least one eye to check. She'd lost count of how many times Snake had retrieved the duvet she kept kicking to the floor. A counsellor once asked her why she needed to be so vigilant? Some secrets were too hard to share.

His voice soothed her frayed nerves, assured her no demon would get within an inch of her. Not on his watch. The rest of the night, Snake slept by her bed, his large hands stroking her forehead, pressing water to her parched lips.

The gentleness of his touch shouldn't surprise her, but the way those caring fingers kneaded the tight knots inside and outside her body made her tense. Go figure. She needed to escape the emotional rollercoaster before she crashed.

Snake had slept in the chair, and judging by the way his chin hung twisted across his chest, plus the awkward angle of the leg tucked under the chair, meant he'd suffer the headache from hell when he woke.

What might it be like to spend the entire morning watching the rise and fall of his massive chest? Torture. With a sigh, she kicked off the duvet and lifted her legs off the bed.

Ouch. With one hand, she poked her cheek, gingerly wiggled her jaw, and waited for the pinpricks of light jiggling around the room to settle. Baxter hadn't pulled his punch. He'd belted her hard. Add the constant throbbing in her ankle, and the day hadn't started well.

"You're awake."

Great. Once a soldier, always a soldier. Although technically ex-SAS were airmen. Snake's reflexes had kicked in as soon as she moved. Mad at herself for setting up the confrontation, she flashed him her best angry bear look. An impersonation she saved for getting rid of lovers who'd overstayed their welcome. Except Snake was not her lover. She rolled her lips and swallowed the wicked possibilities flooding her body.

To Snake's credit, he blinked several times before laughing, and Sam couldn't help appreciating the warm chest rumble that made his blue eyes sparkle. Cue Snake leaving before she did something she'd regret. Unexpected, the tip of his finger stroking her lips, but when did she ever step away from a challenge?

A different story might have unfolded if she hadn't felt worse than awful. If he wasn't Lily's friend, she might have risked serious injury and jumped his bones, spent the next hour or two stoking the fire he lit inside her.

But the goblin with a mallet pounding her head made it difficult to see, let alone fuck. Sam shrugged and focused on the physical urge within her control. "I have to pee."

When he offered to help her out of bed, she showed him the hand. "It's okay. I can manage."

No argument, if she didn't count his, *is she for real*, question written all over his face, Not allowing herself a beat to change her mind, she gripped the edge of the mattress and shifted to her feet. Her ankle buckled.

Snake shook his head. The gesture had become a bloody habit whenever he made it within five feet of her.

"Hopping on one leg, you may not make it. Let me help." His confident grin lifted his cheeks.

"No thanks, I'm sure I can handle taking a pee by myself. No need to hang around. I'll beages in the shower," she lied. She'd have to break both her legs before she let him wrestle with her underwear. Far too early in their relationship. *Relationship!*

"Okay, but are you sure you can stand long enough to shower?"

"For goodness' sake, John, I can manage. Before you leave, do something useful. Check and see if anyone else is awake. Make them coffee. If there's time, check on the dogs. Please."

"Yes, sir, ma'am, sir. Sing out if you need me."

"Will do. Sorry, I'm a grouch at the best of times. Ask Lily, she reckons it's because I spend way too much time on my own bossing around my dogs. She's always suffered from a big case of *you can't handle the truth*." Her best Jack Nicholson impression made no impact. "Not a movie buff? Don't worry, I'll approach human after I shower, clean my teeth. Let me make you breakfast before you head home, and I have to work."

"No need for apologies. Shower. Coffee coming up. By the way, I want to ask you something."

"Oh? Okay." His eyes bored into her as she hobbled to the bathroom, closed the door, and sank on the loo. She had a pretty good idea what he wanted to ask. George had served with honour and courage but no longer had what it took to work for Sentinel. Time for the spaniel to enjoy his well-earned retirement. No problem. Offering Snake's K9 a home would make Bounce the happiest dog on the planet.

Seconds later, she heard a shuffle, and the bathroom door opened a crack. Clothes perched on a disembodied arm floated a foot from the tiled floor.

"Leaving these here for you. Pants, a T-shirt. Boots."

"Thanks. Now go away and leave me in peace." The military-neat pile he offered made her smile. Thoughtful, even if he had forgotten underwear.

"No rush." His reply drifted away from the closed door.

Sam took Snake at his word and slowly wriggled out of her dress. *Ugh.* Like her, it needed a thorough wash. She braced her palms against the shower stall, closed her eyes, and turned on the taps. Warm water beat gently between her shoulder blades, soothing the monster of a dull ache taking over her body.

Reaching for the sponge, she dabbed the tender skin on her cheek. *What the hell was Baxter banging on about?* She'd try to find his damn box, but if she did, he'd be damn lucky if she didn't burn it. She should check the area where he'd been working when they shifted the silos. Maybe Jim had found it and tucked it away somewhere?

Head resting against the tiled wall, she finally worked up the energy to turn off the taps, reach for a towel, dry and get dressed. One leg got caught in her pants. Her hand shot out to grab the edge of the sink before she fell. She should have taken Snake up on his offer, let him help. Luckily, her Ms Sensible side had kept her from what would certainly have led to sex.

The high-pitched scream of a ready kettle tore through her fantasy. The relaxing warmth of the shower swiftly dissipated. An icy blanket threatened to smother her. *Far out. Breathe. This is not Afghanistan.* Repeating the words, she shoved her swollen foot into her boot, held her breath, stumbled down the stairs, and headed for coffee.

"You okay with tea?" Snake asked. "I couldn't find any coffee." His rich baritone grumbled from the veranda.

"Yes. Tea is fine. Is anyone else up?"

"Hate to disappoint you, but the others are gone. Lily left you a note. Go figure. Apparently..." Snake chuckled. "Sentinel business stops for no man, woman, or party."

"So I hear." And the sooner he followed, the better. "I'll join you in a minute. Let me find a bra. Then we can talk." The dogs didn't stir, content to snooze at Snake's feet.

By the time she limped up to the bedroom and back, Miracle Man had returned to the kitchen and put breakfast on the table. Eggs, bacon, toast. Delicious. At five in the morning, when she usually started work, she inhaled a bowl of cornflakes. Most days, the sugary carbohydrate kept her going until she stopped for lunch.

"Sit. How do you have your tea? Milk, sugar?"

Dressed in jeans and a denim shirt that flattered his biceps, a miracle given they were stand-alone extraordinary, Snake stood beside the fridge waving a carton. "Just a splash of milk, no sugar, thanks."

"How's the face?" he asked.

Suddenly feeling claustrophobic from Snake's constant concern, she trembled and grabbed the closest seat. Noses pressed against the mesh screen, Bounce and George barked. "Face is better than I thought it would be. Did you feed the dogs?" she asked trying to keep the shake out of her voice.

"Sure did. Dogs, all good. You said no milk, right?"

"Yes." Sam dipped her chin and jabbed her finger at the awesome breakfast he'd prepared. "Lily told me Spanner had a reputation as Sentinel's in-house chef. I didn't realise he had an apprentice."

Snake's eyes narrowed. "Not me. Blame it on growing up in the childcare system and a string of foster mums insisting if you can boil an egg, you'll never starve."

Sam waved her fork over her plate. "This is more than a boiled egg."

"True. If it's too much, leave it." With a smirk, he reached for her plate.

"No. This is fine. Wouldn't want to put you to any trouble." Her arms flew from beneath the table and circled the plate.

It could have been a trick of the light filtering through the slats in the window shade, but his pale blue eyes glinted. Full of mischief. Okay, her behaviour resembled a contrary five-year-old, but before she could decide whether to apologise again, Snake had slipped his arm around her hunched shoulders. His lips were much too close to her ear. "Be a good girl and drink your tea," he whispered.

Bounce and George yipped encouragement. "What's with the frickin' canine chorus?" *Traitors.*

Snake's mouth hovered over the pulse point at the side of her neck. "Anything else I can get you?"

"Hey!" She nudged his chin, curbing her grin at his long-suffering exhale as he shifted to the seat opposite.

"What have you got planned today? Best not to put too much weight on that ankle. Can I do anything to help?" he asked.

A kind offer, considering she'd been nothing but a bitch. Would it hurt to let her guard down for a couple of hours? "Thanks. I planned to finish moving the last silo. Thought I'd look for Baxter's bloody bag, before I set up the training shed with scents so I can start work with the dogs. They've pretty much sussed my favourite places. Another take on hiding the training lures could be useful, but don't you have to leave?"

"Yes, but I've got a couple of hours. Eat up. Sounds like a busy morning."

Unlike Snake, who tucked into his bacon and eggs as though it were his last meal, Sam had no appetite. Her jaw was much too sore to open wide enough for a decent bite.

Snake's hand stretched across the table. Ignoring the butterflies playing havoc with her stomach, she followed his lead, intertwined her fingers with his, and accepted his reassuring squeeze. Swallowing the lump in her throat took a couple of goes, but eventually she managed it and nodded at Bounce. "She'll keep George in check while we work."

"Yep. The women here have us men well under control."

"You wish." Sam picked up their plates and shuffled to the sink. Not wanting the ants to feast on their leftovers, she insisted on washing up while Snake finished packing. "Go on. Stop fussing. If you think I'm cranky now, wait for it."

"I don't think you're cranky, Sam. Defensive, yes. Although I can't for the life of me figure out why."

The loaded comment tossed over his shoulder unnerved her, but her nervous laugh didn't faze him. "Nothing to figure out. By the way, George can count on a home here with Bounce. If that's what you want?"

"Thanks. Appreciate it. How did you know I planned to ask?" His voice came out scratchy around the edges.

Last time she'd seen him like this, he'd been cradling George in his arms, watching him bleed to death. Sam ran her finger along the ridge of his firm jaw line. "Mind reader, I guess. You can visit whenever you want."

This close, their lips almost touched. She let out a ragged breath, ducked and weaved. "Where's my bloody boots?"

"Slow down, let me help," Snake offered.

"Stop treating me as though I'm a frickin' child. In case you haven't noticed, I'm well over twenty-one, and thanks to the army, I can take care of myself." *Shit.* Someone please tell her to stop, show her how to get rid of the anger constantly forcing her to push people, Snake, away.

"Can't argue with that, but you should ice your face before we get cracking."

Of all the conceited, asinine words he could use? *Should…*

"Well, I think you *should* go shove your head up your arse. Oh, sorry, it's already there." The screen door crashed behind her.

CHAPTER TWELVE

No help from Sam, but he eventually figured out where she kept her supplies and the boxes with the scent lures. He released the safety box lid, loving the noise it made slamming shut. Sam sure knew which button to push to piss him the hell off.

Somewhere in the last twenty-four hours, he'd kissed his brain goodbye. He should be halfway up the M1 heading for a beer, maybe giving Elise a call. Her last text said she was in London, looking to catch up. But leaving in a huff might make Sam's day, and he wasn't feeling particularly agreeable.

Not yet, not until he found out exactly why Sam insisted on pushing him away. *Hell, lover boy, perhaps she's not into you.*

He swallowed hard a few times and shifted focus to what should be the most important thing on his mind. George. Every time he imagined starting his day without him, a boulder the size of the chip on Sam's shoulder perched in the middle of his chest.

He hadn't been there when Mike died, but his pathological need to prove he belonged with his new team had motivated him to volunteer to take on his dog. Since they'd left active service and formed Sentinel, they had been on the trail of Mike's killer, Seckou, and after two years of tracking the bastard, they had him in their sights. George should be there to lick up the mongrel's blood. Victory wouldn't be the same without his mate's dribbly smiles.

Gathering up the scents, Snake wandered outside. George did his best to keep up, but like the brunette busy pushing a silo into place, it proved difficult to do hopping on one leg.

"Ouch." Sam gasped, stepping to the side in time to avoid the teetering silo poised to knock her flat.

"Hey. Let me do that." Patience had never been his strong streak. Sam's head shake and petulant shrug got the better of him. He snatched her wrist and spun her to face him. "This bullshit with your ankle is ridiculous. Where's the local hospital? It's time to get that ankle X-rayed. I'll drive."

"No need. Go ahead and shift the silo while I fetch the other dogs. Bounce, come."

As always, he never gripped her so hard she couldn't escape, but she made a show of wrenching free. "Up to you. But you could have a hairline fracture. Left undetected, it will get worse. Before I leave this afternoon, you will ice it and I will re-strap."

Sam wriggled to her full height. *Here it comes.* Her stubbornness might be funny if he wasn't genuinely concerned. He braced, prepared to show her he didn't intend to retract his order.

"There are an awful lot of personal pronouns in there, John. If you think for one minute, I will…" Bounce huffed a doggy sigh when her phone interrupted.

Grateful the break from the grammar lesson, he sucked in a much-needed breath and turned to give her space, but the light touch of her palm on his shoulder stopped him.

"May I?" She hooked one forearm under his, tapped the speaker button on her phone, and held it in front of her.

For a moment, he got it, help had to be on her terms, but he didn't dare hold it as a certainty. Hell, he got fucking motion sick zigzagging through the signals this crazy woman doled out most of the time. He'd give her the morning. George deserved a proper goodbye.

"Hi Jenna, you're on speaker. What's up? Is Tom okay?"

Snake raised an eyebrow. Tom?

"Hi, Sam. Yes, he's fine, and I know you two aren't supposed to catch up with each other until tomorrow, but can he come over now?"

He didn't recognise the female voice. Could Tom be a dog?

"Yes, no problem. He can help with training. I have a friend here, too."

"Great. Sorry to ask at such short notice. Mountain Rescue called. Can he stay the night? There's an elderly couple missing in *Cleatop Park*."

"Sure. No problem. Have him pack the usual. Include his toothbrush this time." She laughed.

So, he wasn't a dog? Snake raised his other eyebrow. Sam smiled, not willing to let him off the hook.

"Thanks. We'll be there soon."

Sam ended the call, slipped her phone into her pocket, and he felt all kind of good when she kept hold of his arm. Her small hand, the thin line of working dirt beneath her short fingernails, peeked from under his elbow. "Who's Tom?"

"The best looking male I've ever met." She added a sigh, and his heart fell asleep. Her thumb stroked the bend in his elbow. "Don't be a dick, Snake. Tom is thirteen. Jenna, his mum, is a doc. Both of us volunteer at the local branch of Mountain Rescue. When we're not called out together, Tom stays here with me and Bounce. The dogs love him." Her free hand thumped him in the chest. "Me too."

Oxygen finally made it all the way into his lungs when the smile he'd been hanging for beamed his way.

Mindful of Sam's ankle, he tightened his hold on her arm, silently hoping she wouldn't pull away, and grabbed the scent boxes. As they walked to the training barn, he asked if she'd found Baxter's toolbox.

"No. I looked but didn't find anything. Jim missed the party, but I must remember to check with him." Sam let go of his arm and limped over to various straps, ropes, and bits of equipment hanging on a row of pegs. When she stretched for a harness on the top hook, he stepped forward and reached for it. Anything to make her life easier.

A hint of lace flashed through the gap in her shirt and his cock was instantly hard, jealous of the material caressing Sam's flawless skin. One of his foster mothers would have described the colour of the lace as aqua and ordered her boy to lower his gaze. The libido-charged man standing here now couldn't take his eyes off Sam's perfect breasts.

"Snake. Catch." Sam hopped on her uninjured leg, flipped the harness, and tossed it his way.

Bounce tilted her head to the side, her dark brown eyes full of more than questions. "What?" The dog's head flipped to the other side. "Cocky girl. Come on. We've got work to do."

The morning went quickly. Hanging with Snake had been fun and productive, even if she couldn't get her head around spending more time with him. When he was anywhere close, she felt less stressed than she remembered being in a long time, her mind and body relaxed. Sensations buried with Ed came to life. The intimate shivering deep in her pelvis whenever Snake brushed against her.

Snake had a way with dogs, which didn't surprise her after witnessing his bond with George, but for a man who obviously enjoyed being in control, he had taken a back seat. Most of the time. The scent training interested him. They'd fallen into an easy rhythm, and after the bullshit with Baxter, she had to admit his concern for her dumb ankle was more welcome than comfortable.

After running the dogs through their paces, they headed in for lunch, arriving at the house in time to see Tom storming up the driveway, Jenna following slowly behind him in her car.

Snake raised his eyebrows and tilted his head at the pair. "That Tom? He doesn't look happy."

"No," she agreed, and frowned. Like most teenagers, Tom could be moody. But most of the time, he got on well with his mum. Unless Baxter was home. Then the lad stayed in his room, keeping out of his way.

Clouds swirled overhead. Despite the sun being out most of the morning, thawing the snow, the bitter chill from yesterday had returned, making her eyes water. She smiled. At least she didn't have to pour her body into that party dress. They were in for another storm today.

CHAPTER THIRTEEN

Arms pinned to his side, standing straighter than a soldier on parade, Tom's bottom lip trembled. Sam coughed, struggling not to take on the lad's bag-of-sad. Time to move this along before she dissolved into teary mush. The teenager reminded her of Arash. Older, but small for his age. They shared an identical stubborn streak. Even if a tsunami swamped the earth, neither kid would budge.

Quiet by nature, tears glistened in Jenna's eyes. Daily, the single mum struggled to keep her son in line. To make matters worse, Jenna had shacked up with that piece of shit, Baxter, making her volatile relationship with Tom worse. But every time Sam tried talking to her, Jenna fobbed her off, not wanting to hear anything negative when it came to her man. The jerk had played on her loneliness, inserted himself into their home, before her friends suspected he had an agenda that didn't include her teenage son.

Deep down, Tom adored his mum, and until Baxter had moved in, he had been Jenna's rock. Then things went tits up and Tom started acting out. "Please, love. I'm sorry. Promise I will make it up to you. I love you." The sadness in Jenna's voice was palpable. Unfortunately, nothing got through to the pissed off teenager who had no problem showing Mum their retreating behind. Rude, and more than Jenna deserved.

Sam closed her eyes and exhaled. Pulling them in for a group hug might seem like a first-class idea, but she didn't dare risk it. Behind her, the wall of solid muscle shifted. Tom crossed his arms and dug his chin deep into his chest. He hated sports, preferred a book to a ball. Bad luck for Tom. His dad had been a school champion. Part of the reason for his over-the-top reaction. Determined to prove he could shine at physical stuff, too. Tomorrow he intended to shine on the annual sports day, show Jenna how much he had improved.

The bruises and scabs on his knees were evidence of how much tomorrow meant to him. Battle scars earned during weeks of after-school training perfecting his skills.

Jenna stepped off the veranda and took a few steps towards the glowering boy. *That took guts.*

"I want to be there, you know I do, but people need me."

"*I* need you," Tom whined. Bounce flicked his ears. The lad's voice was shrill, half-way from breaking from boy to man.

"Enough." Snake beat Sam to it, his tone quiet, but inviting no come back.

Salty tears burned Sam's eyes. Mother and son altercations had been a definite weak spot even before Afghanistan. If she didn't act fast, she'd make a complete plonker of herself. "Hey, Tom. I'd appreciate you hanging with us tonight. You're amazing with Meadow, and her pups are busting to come into this world. I'd say tonight's the night." She'd been expecting the Malinois to go into labour for the last twenty-four hours.

Tom glared at her. "Sorry, Sam. I don't want to stay here. You have shit internet. I can't run my games."

Tom often stayed at her place when Jenna had a call-out. Jim slept in a caravan in one of the fields and stepped in if she had to join the rescue, making sure Tom was safe and out of trouble. But she couldn't disagree. On a good day, her internet signal flipped between passable and iffy. *A little help here.* Sam dug the tip of her elbow into Snake's ribs. Of course, the big lug didn't flinch.

Snake cleared his throat. "Hey, buddy. Relax."

Tom squared off with the man behind her. Kid had balls.

Jenna interrupted the testosterone face-off. "I had no warning. They called when you were eating breakfast."

"I don't believe you," Tom replied, kicking the dirt with the toe of his boot.

"It's true. Why would I lie?" Jenna took a step closer to her son.

Hands in his pockets, shoulders hunched, Tom stared at the ground. Pizza for dinner didn't guarantee he'd feel any better. Her last hope hung on the ice cream left over from Lily's party.

"Can't someone else go?" Tom whined.

Fuck. The kid was set to drag the heart right out of her chest.

Jenna shook her head, bracing for incoming defeat. "I realise this game means a lot to you. It's hard, but if I don't make it, Sam will be there tomorrow. Won't you?"

Guess so. Resigned to testing her proxy parenting skills, she nodded. "You bet. Wouldn't miss it. Snake will be there too, right?" Snake grunted. "He used to play…"

"No offence, Sam, but it's not the same," Tom dismissed her bonding myth.

She swiped the back of her hand across her mouth to hide her chuckle. Definitely on a roll, and if he kept it up, he might break his mum. "Well. Don't know about you, but I'm freezing. You best get moving, Jenna. Let's go inside, mate. There's pizza in the fridge." Sam twitted on, trying to diffuse the situation. Negotiating with the Taliban had been easier. "Tom, didn't you need a badge sewn on your guernsey?"

Snake cleared his throat. His eyebrow quirked. What? He doubted her needlework skills?

"Sam's *magic* at sewing," Tom said.

"I'm sure she is." Jenna hiccupped. "Look, I understand you're disappointed, upset, but you're not a baby, Tom. I expect you to handle this."

"I thought he was doing brilliantly," Snake mumbled beside her, earning himself another dig in the ribs.

Obviously entertained by the drama, Snake looked down at her and smiled. "Shh. This is serious."

"There will be other matches." Jenna sniffed.

"You best get going, Jenna. He'll be okay." Snake interrupted before round two started.

Thank you, Sam mouthed.

"Sure he will." Jenna turned to her son. "I love you, baby."

"I don't care."

"Right then, hot drinks coming up. There's a ton of cake left over from the party. Tom, give your mum a hug. Now the nights are getting colder, and we're expecting more snow, I'm worried for Meadow. Let's go make sure she's comfortable, and then you can show me how to play that FIFA game. If the internet is a pain, we can play Monopoly. Yes?" Sam held her breath, praying Snake agreed to join them, but when Tom declared Monopoly the dumbest game ever, she could swear Snake winked.

You thought the bear was bad. Try the death stare.

"That sounds great, baby. You used to love playing with dad." Tears shone in Jenna's eyes and Sam wished she'd never mentioned the damn game. Why did she have to mention the game? "You'll want to get an early night. Be fresh for the game tomorrow."

"Stuff the game."

"But the team is depending on you?"

Not prepared to go another round, Sam took her hands out of her pockets and shoved open the door.

"Hey, big man. Don't know how long you've been playing FIFA, but I'm sure I can beat you," Snake said.

"You're full of shit."

"Nope. Try me."

Sam sighed. She owed Snake big time and had a thousand ways

she'd love to show her appreciation. Everything from kissing that sexy mouth to sucking his toes. *Hell.* She didn't remember ever having such an over-the-top, instant reaction to any man. Pleasant? Could be.

Her pelvis tingled. All fairy dust and rabid lust. Her snicker earned her a few raised eyebrows, but it didn't deter Tom, who showed sterling grit and refused to say goodbye. Tough to the end.

Jenna waved and headed towards her car. "Bye. What's the odds I'll get there and find the missing pair shrouded in blankets enjoying a hot cuppa? I could be home in a couple of hours." She aimed the last sentence at Tom. "Thanks, Sam, you're an angel. I'll phone tomorrow. You can give me a play-by-play of the game."

Jeez! Jenna. Champion of the brave face. Nowhere near as strong, Sam flicked the moisture from her cheek. Snake's fingers curled around her shoulders and in a moment of weakness, her forehead sank into his chest.

Slowly, he angled her to the door. "You two go inside and get warm. I'll put some water up for the dogs."

"Thanks. I appreciate it." Sam watched him stride away. His long legs pawed the ground as the dogs trotted behind their alpha. She smiled. Sexy and kind. A winning combination.

CHAPTER FOURTEEN

Fine by him. Leaving Tom with Sam, taking time out to feed the dogs. No matter how much Sam loved to rattle his cage, Snake meant it when he said he wanted to help.

All morning, before the kid arrived, face deadpan, she had limped around the barn, trying not to wince every time she put weight on her foot. He worried she may have suffered more than a sprain, but he couldn't do much about it if she refused to get it X-rayed. Sam was an adult, not a teenager. *Hah!*

His blood boiled every time he saw the purple bruise on her cheek. A punch to the face hurt like hell for days, robbing you of any sensible thought.

Filling the bucket for the last time, he took a sec to appreciate Sam's impressive set-up. The woman knew her stuff when it came to training dogs. Earlier, when she'd asked him to hide the Kong with the scent, like a kid up for a challenge, he'd done his damndest to find an impossible spot and ended up smiling through his arse. The joke on him. In less than five minutes, her dog found it, sank to the ground, and barked twice. Job done.

Next time, when he visited George, maybe he'd ask if he could hang out for a few days and watch Sam work with the cadaver dogs. Smart animals. Incredibly smart, sexy woman. It was hot the way she assumed the alpha role and commanded Bounce through her paces. The German shepherd was something else. No wonder George had fallen in love.

What he didn't get? Her drive to unleash her grouch on anyone who paid her a compliment, god forbid praised her impressive skills. No one spared except Lily. Snake propped his arse against the fence and stroked his chin. Yeah, nah. Could he be the only person who rubbed Sam the wrong way? And why the hell did he care? Because he couldn't remember when he'd been this attracted to a woman. Most likely more to do with her being injured—vulnerable. His DNA speaking, wanting to make sure she was okay.

Mystery solved. He shifted off the fence and dug the heel of his boot deep into the mud. For a start, Sam wasn't his type. Too small. In the unlikely event they ever got together, one night he might turn over in bed and crush her. He shuddered, remembering the last time he'd been on top of her at the hotel in Mali.

Thinner than he preferred, too, but not weak. Fit. Her slender legs were long and toned. The definition in her calves a distinct turn on. His brain went AWOL, wandering to a future that featured those legs, a vise around his waist, as he pounded into her.

Any time they got close, her soft curves melted his hard edges, made his blood pressure soar. Sam's breasts were a perfect fit for the palm of his hand. Sam tried hard to hide it, but he had been around enough women to know she found him attractive. Just better than him at holding the boundary. That invisible line—neither of them should cross. Because one night in the sack, no matter how mind-blowing, wouldn't be worth the inevitable fallout. The penalty for messing on home turf.

Besides, he'd sworn off dating until Sentinel annihilated Seckou. As the team's comms man, Knight and the others were relying on him to locate the murdering terrorist. So far, he was batting an embarrassing zero.

Back in London, he could take care of his horny cock and focus on his fucking job, but nothing came harder than saying goodbye to George. Mike's dog had been there for him, no questions asked, and it would be hard spending his day without him.

Snake's stomach growled. "Ready for lunch, boy?" George let out a long, satisfied sigh. "None of that kibble shit, ay feller? I'll find you a bone dripping marrow." George closed his eyes. *Yeah.*

Dogs fed, Snake secured the padlock on the kennel door and started back to the house, making a mental note to organise a regular bone drop for George, when the air shifted and the hairs on his neck stood to attention. Beside him, George growled. From nose to tail, every muscle in his body focused in front of them. Snake tugged his collar. "Easy, boy. I see him."

Close to the tree line, partially hidden by a large oak, a man stood watching Sam's house. "Hey, can I help you?" he called, but the guy took off in the opposite direction.

Snake shrugged. As if Sam didn't offer sufficient distraction, he'd started imagining Seckou and his terrorist mates behind every hay bale.

Leaving George must be doing a number on his head. With a four-and-a-half-hour drive down to London, he should eat, play that game of FIFA with Tom, and apologise for not been at his game tomorrow. That wouldn't go down well.

He shrugged and jogged to the house, George galloping awkwardly beside him. Sam, the afternoon sun bouncing off the auburn highlights in her hair, sat with Tom rugged up on the deck. As he got close, the lad stood and shifted behind her. Earlier he'd noticed Tom didn't have a problem with Bounce but was shy around George.

"It's okay, Tom. George is a friendly." Sam stretched her hand out to his dog. "Sit, boy."

Willing to play along, George obliged.

"Like you do with Bounce and Meadow, hold out your hand, palm to the ground, and let him have a sniff."

Snake hung back, content to watch. Sam's gaze met his, her nod barely noticeable, but his heart beat faster. He'd done something right, pleased her, and shit if it didn't feel great.

Tentatively, the boy uncurled his fingers. George's eyes narrowed, a low groan rumbling in his chest. Boy, the dog could ham it up, and for a sec, Snake thought his canine may have gone too far, scarred the boy for life.

"It's okay. He wants to say hello," Sam said, her smile wide enough to share with Tom and George but landing shy of Snake.

Tom did his best not to flinch. Dog took pity on him, sniffed his shaky fingers, and granted the kid a lick. Tom's nervous laugh hit Snake square in the chest. The way it robbed him of breath was nothing like the gunshot that had torn up his lung in Africa. This blow loaded with a gentler power. The kind that changed a man. Snake shuffled his feet.

"You were quick. Have you finished?" Sam asked him, her smile slipping from her face. Pity.

"Yep. All done."

"Did you log in all the unused samples? It's important."

"Aware of that. Logged and signed off."

"Okay. I guess it's time to eat. Hungry?"

The boy nodded. That made the two of them. "You expecting visitors?" Snake tipped his chin toward to where he'd seen the stranger.

"What makes you say that?"

"I saw a guy over by the barn. Thought he might be looking for you."

Sam sprang to her feet and hopped. "Baxter. I'll…"

The kid's eyes went wide as saucers. "Take it easy. It's not him." Snake assured her and scraped the mud from his boots on the edge of the step. "Hey, Tom. What do you think of my three-legged pal?" He flicked his gaze at George, who had one of his paws firmly on the boy's foot.

"Okay?" Tom's eyes darted from Sam out along the path.

Teenagers usually had more to say for themselves. Small for his age. Perhaps they bullied him at school? He recognized the signs. He had been quiet at school, but unlike Tom, his physical size meant from the get-go no one ever picked on him. "Tom, let's see if we can get Sam's computer going. I feel a win coming on."

"Sure. Okay." The lad returned Snake's 'high five' and the rush from earlier crept up his spine.

Sam smiled that smile, the one that went on automatic recall when it met him. "You go on in, Tom. I'll be there in a minute after I check and make sure Snake's done everything he's supposed to."

Snake sucked in a breath. For sure, Sam taking off for the barn was odd, but she didn't plan on adding him in on any sitrep. She certainly didn't need to know how much her not trusting him hurt. He only hoped she didn't have any plans to go after the stranger.

"Where did you say you saw our visitor?" Sam asked, her head swivelling right and left.

"Over by the barn. Something wrong?"

Tom tugged on Sam's sleeve. "Can I take George inside with me?"

"Sorry, Tom, George stays. But you can bring your lunch out here and keep him and Bounce company. Okay?"

Snake said nothing, split between supporting her on her no dogs in the house rule and wanting to understand why this guy had her this bloody concerned.

George whimpered, but Sam didn't flinch. Snake stifled a chuckle. As a card-carrying member of his family, unless George was in harness, working, Snake couldn't deny him anything.

"Come on, champ. Don't know about you, but I'm starving. The dogs can chill while we get something to eat." Snake placed his hands on the lad's shoulders and pointed him at the door. "Go on in and get stuck into Sam's fridge. I'll be right there."

Tom dragged his foot away from George's paw, who whined with disappointment. Snake gave him a pat and twirled his tongue over his top teeth. The boy tugged deep. He watched him disappear before grabbing Sam's forearm. "You want to tell me what's with our visitor?"

She glared at his hand. He released his grip. Staying close, Snake tilted his head, waiting for her to elaborate. When she didn't and stepped off the patio, heading toward the trees, he had to ask. "Want me to come with you?"

"Nope and nope." Miss Independent hobbled away. Her arse swayed sexily in her worn blue jeans.

Fine. He irritated her. Had done ever since his flying leap decked her in Mali. Lunch—leave. A trained soldier, Sam could take care of herself. And he didn't need the ego bashing.

She didn't make it three feet before her phone beeped. "Oh hell." Phone to her ear, Sam dug her heel in the snow.

"What is it?" Snake asked.

"Rescue HQ. Snow is hampering the search. They need Bounce."

"Go. I've got Tom," he said, no hesitation. Didn't matter how many times he tried to get his act on the road, he was right where he should be.

"I'm on my way." Sam hung up. "Thanks, but I've held you up too long. Call Jim. His number's on the fridge. He'll take over. Tell him, with any luck, I'll only be gone for a few hours."

"Yeah, yeah. Go." They both knew luck had nothing to do with inexperienced people surviving bad weather.

Snake waited for her to fetch warm weather gear from the house, followed her to her vehicle, and opened the door. Her right eyebrow arched as he took her elbow and helped her into the driver's seat. His gaze drifted to her bung ankle, unsurprised when her eye roll responded.

Snake shut the door, put the key in the ignition, rolled down his window, and waited for Sam to blast him for being an overprotective control freak. He blew a sigh of relief into the frigid air when she waved and smiled.

"Bye, Snake. Appreciate your help. Drive safely. See you some-time. Call anytime for a George update."

He waited until the vehicle vanished through the trees, behind a curtain of snow. Another night in Giggleswick. *Fantastic.* Snake ran his fingers through his damp hair and grunted, hoping to hell FIFA kept the cranky teenager entertained.

CHAPTER FIFTEEN

"Stop. Take a breath, mate, and consider the next words to come out of your mouth."

Snake had no intention of indulging a kid, itching to take his anger out on someone—anyone. A thirteen-year-old struggling with his new testosterone levels didn't need his level of confrontation. Snake couldn't resist a growl and ducked his head in the fridge for the sandwich stuff cocky pants had refused to find.

"Look, mister."

"Snake. Name's Snake, or John." He grabbed the left-over pizza off the shelf and reached for the bottle of coke.

"Bet you wouldn't appreciate it if your mum preferred being with other people on the most important day of your life? She couldn't care less." The kid vented with the drama harnessed, especially for teens.

"Didn't your dad ever tell you? Always show your mother respect." Okay, harsh playing the dead parent card, but he'd had a gut full of the whining.

"Whatever. While we're at it, what kind of handle is Snake?"

"Military nickname. Everyone has them." He placed the leftovers on the table and batted the kid's hand when he made a grab for the slice of pizza closest to Snake. "Manners."

"What? You want to say a prayer or something?"

"Not me. But have at it." The chair screeched as Snake pulled it from under the table.

"So, how did you get your name? Slithering your way into places you shouldn't, I bet."

"Kind of."

Tom grabbed another slice and piled it on top of the first. Certain there'd be more attempts to get up his nose, Snake took a deep breath and let that one go to the keeper.

"Okay. How, then?"

Since leaving active duty, he'd avoided discussing his military service, but this might be the way to make a friend and earn a less fractured evening later. He reached into his pocket for his mobile. "See this. A phone, right? Well, I programmed it with a heap of code that lets me get into places no one else knows exist. Proved very useful in combat."

"Wicked." Tom crossed his arms over his chest and cocked his head to one side. "Are you one of those computer geeks?"

"Kind of. A comms man. What about you? Your school mates give you a name?"

"No, but…"

He hadn't expected the lad's cheeks to flush or silence to smother the kitchen. "Understood. Prefer not to share. Ready for ice cream?"

"Sure."

He collected the tub from the freezer and wandered over to where Tom had set up the game.

"Are you great at this, or were you talking yourself up in front of your girlfriend?"

"Try me. And Sam isn't my girlfriend."

"Could have fooled me, the way you were looking at her this morning. I bet you're dying to get in her pants."

Tom's smirk hit a nerve. "Watch your mouth. Spitfire." The kid may have a ton of emotional stuff going on, but he wouldn't tolerate him disrespecting Sam or his mother.

Tom's arms tightened around his chest and his chin jutted forward. "Spitfire? Now who's calling people names?"

"Your mouth has a habit of running away from you. I figure the nickname suits. But if you object, fair enough."

Tom grabbed one spoon and dug deep into the carton. "No. S'okay."

Snake grabbed the other spoon as Tom went for his second helping. Their spoons clashed. He waited for the explosion, but none came. Instead, the kid's laugh tore at his gut. "Did you check if the internet is working?"

"Yeah. All good."

"Okay. I've got these." Snake grabbed their plates and the empty pizza box.

Tom returned his wink. While he stood in the kitchen, Snake checked his phone. No word from Sam. No reason he should expect any, but he worried her ankle might not hold up for long. Add the weather. The mysterious knob he'd seen earlier. In particular, the latter shook his trouble antenna.

"Shift over." Snake sat beside the boy. "Okay, Spitfire, let's see what you got. Later, we'll check on Meadow and George."

Sleet and snow crisscrossed the moor, hampering the search and making it damn difficult for Bounce. But the canine star refused to give up searching until she caught a whiff of the couple's scent. Less than an hour later, she sank to her haunches in the snow and barked once. Her signal. Couple found. Never tired of seeing her wagging tail, Sam tossed Bounce her favourite toy. Small reward for a massive job.

The hikers were alive. Hypothermic, a few cuts and bruises, but no major injuries. Lucky, considering they had ventured onto the dales ill-equipped, telling no one where they were going. According to the tourist websites, the terrain ranked among England's most picturesque. Conveniently, they forgot one bit, the warning of how quickly the dales could turn deadly. Especially on nights like the last few.

By the time she got home, parked her vehicle, and bedded Bounce down, it was nearly two a.m. Happy to see his friend, George gave her his best doggy smile and shared his warm spot in the hay.

Sam pointed her feet at the house, hoping they found enough oomph to make it upstairs to her bed. During the search, her ankle had held up, but the persistent throb unsettled her stomach. Since she had convinced Jenna to let Tom stay the night, she checked they weren't still up and glued to their computer screens.

No lights were on in the living room, so she kicked off her shoes and tiptoed to the spare room crammed with unpacked boxes and a sleeping mat. Tom's fave place to sleep. Since she'd left home at seventeen, she'd trekked the growing assortment of vital rubbish from place to place, but certain items never found a permanent home.

A quick peck on his forehead satisfied the heart reaching for him as she brushed the hair from his eyes. Recently, he'd lost his way, angry at everyone. Easy to relate. She backed out of the room, unable to take her eyes off him, until the door clicked shut.

A cup of cocoa sounded perfect, but to get to the kitchen, she'd have to go through the living room where Snake slept on the sofa.

One leg bent, foot flat on the floor, his arm supported his neck at an awkward angle. His black cotton T-shirt pulled tight across the hard lines of his muscular pecs. She winced. His neck would hurt in the morning.

Resting her elbows on the back of the sofa, she ogled the rise and fall of his snoring chest. With his spidey skills, she had no hope of getting close without waking him. Without warning, his eyes opened. His gaze as warm as the embers of the dying fire fixed on her.

"Hey. Everything okay?" His sleepy drawl soothed the ridges of her soul better than any mug of hot chocolate.

"Yeah. Both are alive, which is more than I can say for the end of my nose. Cold as a witch's tit."

"Mmm. Interesting picture." Snake swung his other leg off the sofa and patted the spot beside him. "Sit. How's the ankle? Let me get you something hot to drink."

"No, thanks. All good." Her fingers skimmed his as she flopped beside him. The warmth of his skin sent shivers skittering across her forearms.

In a flash, he tore the shawl from the sofa and draped it over her shoulders. "About that hot drink."

"Okay. Stop nagging. I think there's something stronger in the cupboard above the fridge."

"Coming up." He reached for her feet and swung them onto the sofa. "Relax. Get warm. I'll give the fire a stoke."

A smile crept over her face. Happy to watch his sexy butt as he bent over and kept his word, a smile crept over her face. "Take all the time you need." Too soon he wandered off to the kitchen and returned with two glasses of the whisky she kept for special occasions. "Thanks."

He placed his on the small coffee table, reached for her left foot, and cradled it in his massive hands. Strong hands sent from heaven. Should she resist? Probably, but the moonlight danced through the lace curtains and flitted over the long fingers kneading her arches. A deep groan escaped her lips. "Sorry."

"Why?"

Fuck knew. In fact, what other moves did he have to make her moan? She'd need another lifetime to explore this man's bag of tricks. She checked herself. Her capacity for sharing didn't include giving in to the invitation in his blue eyes.

Her breath caught. Had to be the unexpected kickback of the whisky. "Wow, this stuff is powerful." She coughed, and the glass slipped from her hand spilling the drink onto the carpet. "Damn."

Snake's arm curled around her waist.

"Leave it," he ordered. "It's been a long night. Time for bed."

Tempting to melt into the magic of his words. Her head fell against his chest. The solid wall of muscle a perfect pillow. Sam's eyes fluttered closed. "Must be the whisky," she muttered, her voice drifting away.

"Must be. It's late, you're tired, and we both need sleep."

Halfway up the stairs, her toes levelled with the horizon. Airborne. Swept off her feet again. *No.* No way did she intend falling for Snake, and now was a perfect time to put him straight. "John. We must talk."

"In the morning."

The light on the landing was a mix of misty purple and blue, but she ignored the dawn and sank deeper into him. He smelled of dog and pizza. The sexiest scent ever. She sighed.

CHAPTER SIXTEEN

Pacing back and forth, waiting for Sam to come home, playing Mr Mum to Spitfire had not been how Snake envisaged yesterday panning out, but hanging with the kid hadn't ended up half as bad as he feared. The kid beat him fair and square at FIFA, and for a couple of hours, they'd both chilled.

Sam turned in her sleep and moaned. Fists battling invisible enemies, she'd been restless ever since he carried her to bed. "Shh. Go to sleep." Stretching across her body, careful not to make contact, he eased the duvet over her pale shoulder and cursed the familiar swelling in the front of his jeans. Permanently hard for her since Lily's party. He put it down to lack of sex, something he planned on taking care of as soon as he made it back to London.

Simple stuff, like standing next to Sam, shielding her from the wind, made him horny. But one thing for sure, guarding the petite woman ranked as a hell of a lot more important than convincing her to let him in her pants. *Keep telling yourself that.*

After Sam cried out for the tenth time that night, he parked his arse in his seat by the draughty window. Something intruded and disturbed her sleep, and deep creases marred her pretty forehead.

One hundred to one, Snake bet it had everything to do with the stranger nosing around her property.

But the defensiveness, stubborn independence, bouncing off her in waves took years to perfect. A person's past shaped their moods and moulded attitude. It didn't take Freud to see Sam's fear in the not-so-subtle dip of the chin. Eyes that took an interest in anything other than his fucking face.

He just prayed he didn't scare her, but if he did, he had a hundred ways to soothe her nightmares. Replace the scary dark with pleasure instead of pain. Unfortunately, many of his treatment plans began with joining her in that bed and spooning her to him. Pity he didn't have an invitation.

Not likely to get one. The thought triggered an unfamiliar uneasiness, but he'd learnt a long time ago not to question his instincts. A master at reigning in emotion, he'd respect her choice, never force her to share her body or her shadows. But if he used a little charm? Wore her down until she trusted him as a friend who treasured her and who'd obliterate mountains for her smile? He'd rise to that challenge if he'd planned to be in England, but earlier, he'd checked his contacts in Burkina, and new intel reported they had eyes on Seckou.

Sure, the temptation to brush it off as another false sighting was strong except, this time, instinct told him they might, just maybe, have cracked the fucker's inner circle. Money talked in every shabby corner of the world, and there must be one of his generals ready to give the bastard up for a fat wad of American dollars.

Not long after they finally dozed off, a sharp knocking on the front door woke them. Immediately, he checked Sam. Light bounced off the highlights in Sam's hair onto her sleepy face and sank into the purple shadow beneath her bruised eye. If, make that when, Snake got his hands on Baxter…

"Shit. Sorry." Sam groaned. "I overslept. It's Jenna. Is Tom awake?"

He lurched out of the chair. "Rest. You had a big night. I'll rouse him."

He didn't have to go far beyond the bottom of the stairs to see the lad shuffling his feet at the front door before Jenna pulled her son into her arms.

"Missed you," she said.

"Me, too," Tom mumbled from her armpit.

"Hi, Snake. Thanks for keeping my man company."

"No problem. Want some coffee?"

"Thanks, but we'd better get going. Big day today. Right?" Tom squirmed at the kiss plonked on his forehead. "Say hi to Sam for me. Tell her I'll call later."

Jenna scrubbed Tom's hair and the old longing rolled in Snake's gut. Thirty years, and he still missed his mother. "Will do." He stepped forward and pumped Tom's fist. "Make sure you're the best man and win."

A half-smile and wink from Tom, a quick wave from Jenna, and her car barrelled off along the road. Snake glanced at his watch. Enough time to make Sam a quick breakfast before he finally got his arse back to London.

Before the air shifted, he sensed Sam standing behind him. "Thought you were staying in bed," he said without turning.

"Thought wrong."

He shrugged. If they were going to go the usual ten rounds, he needed help. "Coffee?" He nudged the door open wider and caught her standing on one leg, one hand resting on the wall for balance.

Three strides and he would have kept on coming if it weren't for her gasp. Instead, he stopped short of giving into temptation and planting his lips on hers. "Sorry." A thousand thoughts swam in his head. Hard to tell which one deserved the apology.

Heart thumping, tension building in every muscle, Snake didn't take his eyes off Sam as he scanned for her usual no-touch warning. When she didn't flinch, he hooked his index finger over the waistband of her jeans.

"I have a question, Ms Leigh. George is a fussy eater. What do you feed your dogs?"

Sam blinked; her long eyelashes flicked her high cheekbones. "Kibble."

"Treats?" he asked. Damn near losing his mind, he undid the button of her jeans, tugged on the zipper, checking for those signs, and slid his palm smoothly inside her pants.

A low moan escaped her plush lips before she clasped his wrists. Her tight grasp slowed fingers, eager to explore. "Treats?" Sam's mouth curled in a Mona Lisa, all kinds of knowing smile, and her good eye twinkled. The other winced, if that was possible. "An occasional bone."

Now we're talking. "Perfect," Snake mumbled.

"Glad we agree." She licked her lips and circled her hips.

Small, undulating movements that set his blood on fire. His gaze stayed on a mouth overflowing with promise. "Stuff could get complicated," he warned as Sam's delicate fingers traced the line of his pec through his denim shirt. *Sex is always complicated.* He wondered what brought on her sudden willingness to be this close. Not for long.

"I'm not expecting commitment, Snake. But it's been a shit couple of days. I need a kiss."

Her honesty. A fucking aphrodisiac. A signal he didn't need to worry. Sam wasn't into the emotional bullshit many women he'd met excelled at. A forever he couldn't give. Funny, but Sam's breathy assurance left him wishing, this time, things might be different.

"But if you're seeing someone I... Is there anyone?" She lightly pinched his erect nipple.

"No." An audible groan as her fingers fluttered over his abs. Apparently, Sam liked to tease, and fuck him if it didn't turn him on. He longed to bring her the pleasure she deserved.

"Then we have no problem?" Her hand slid over the front of his jeans and gripped his erection.

"Sam. Don't," he warned.

She drew her hand away. "Please."

"Be sure." He grabbed her hand and put it back where it belonged, cupping his cock.

"Sure." Her turn to fiddle with the zip.

His mouth fell on hers, possessive, demanding. If he came on strong, she might decide kissing screamed dumb idea and tell him to back the hell off and give them both time to think.

Gutsy as hell, Sam rose onto her toes, bit his bottom lip. Her arms reached over his shoulders, pulled him close enough to mould her slim curves to his torso.

"Undo your shirt. I want to see you," he said.

CHAPTER SEVENTEEN

Baxter tightened his grip on Murphy's neck, the pressure leaching the blood from his fingernails. Seeing the tosser's face contorted in agony and defeat ranked as more enjoyable than sex. But considering he'd spent the past six months lying next to Jenna the Jellyfish, listening to her banging on and on about her dead husband, this mother fucker didn't have to work very hard to please.

For fun, he recalled the day he'd told Jenna how things were going to work if she wanted her precious son to stay healthy. Having her tiptoe around the place, flinching when he got within a foot of the boy, was a fantastic reason to get up in the morning. Thank Christ he wouldn't have to play wake up next to Jellyfish for much longer.

Another twist and Murphy's eyes boggled. Baxter's hand turned numb, so he turned it down a notch, but he wanted to make the most of his time while Jenna played doc out on the moor. With any luck, she'd get swallowed up in the snowstorm and save him the trouble of killing her. One positive thing to come out of this whole fucking mess? He wouldn't have to put up with her and the whiny kid much longer. Sayonara. Too fucking long in coming.

He had Sam, the bitch owner of the kennels, to thank. Refusing to return his property, she had ruined his business. Now he needed to get out of Giggle Sick before his supplier caught up with him. First, Sam had to pay. *Time's ticking bitch.* Tonight, he'd take his chances and try to find his drugs. He eyed the bag in the corner that contained the meat for the dogs, laced with shut-eye.

Once he had his stash, no one would find him. A plane to an island paradise, before he spent the rest of his days lounging on a beach, fucking little girls, and sipping cocktails. The perfect life. *Living the dream, Baxter Boy.* And then some until the knob'ed hanging off the end of his arm moaned.

"Please, man," he gurgled.

"What? That's all you got? Please? Fuck me. Nothing else? No, oh, God, this can't be happening?" Baxter's free fist ploughed into Murphy's gut, forcing blood and spit to shoot from his mouth, bounce off his clean shirt, and splattered over the shed floor. He hit Murphy again. The cracking of bones, plus the son of a bitch's pathetic groans, reminded Baxter of one of those computer games the idiot kid played night and day.

"I warned you to keep the fuck out of sight." Baxter let Murphy go and he crumpled to the ground. He kicked the fucker until he curled into a ball. Indulging himself for a sec, he flexed his fingers and admired the bruises and cuts on his knuckles. Badges of commitment.

"Please!"

"Shit, you're boring, Murphy. Get up." Baxter hauled him to his feet and landed another blow to the fucker's jaw. Above his head, a convenient piece of rope swung from a hook. Perfect for stringing Murphy's hands above his shaking head. Dead weight, he was a bitch to lift, thanks to the beating. With his wrists shackled to the hook, he must know it would soon be over, that nothing he could say could save his sad skin.

"One, two." Quick jabs to Murphy's solar plexus. Pissed it didn't rank anywhere near as satisfying as punching the heavy bag at the gym, Baxter raised his fist for another round. A chuckle percolated in his gut until he couldn't hold it down any longer. His laugh erupted, filled the entire shed. Fuck, he loved this new stuff. He rarely sampled the merchandise, but this shit was unbelievable. The rush phenomenal. No wonder the kids lined up for it on a Saturday night.

"Baxter, man. I'm begging you. For fuck's sake..."

"Forget the magic word, Murphy? Come on, let me hear it."

"Please."

Murphy's pathetic whine pissed him off. "Shut your mouth." Baxter planted a swift uppercut to the man's jaw. Broke it, for sure. "Too late, crying now, arsehole. You had one job. One fucking job."

Murphy's head slumped to the side.

"No. Open your fucking eyes." He shook him until snot dripped onto his chin. "You had one job. Stay out of sight in the trees while I searched, and whistle if anyone came close. But no, you had to stick your big fat head out for lover boy."

His blood boiled. His heart bashed against his chest, adrenaline levels soaring. "This is all your fault, Murphy." Unless he wanted to face Ugly Joe, he had no choice but to speed up his exit plan. The fat bastard hadn't gotten his name for nothing. Overdue payments were not an option. He had to retrieve his stash, take care of Jenna and the kid, and leave, but not before he got to the best part. His plan for Sam.

First, he'd clear his head and play a little longer with Murphy. Unfortunately, it wouldn't be as long as he'd like. Defeated, the fuck face didn't have any fight left in him. His eyeballs swam in their sockets. "Lost your tongue, arsehole?" *Now there's a thought.*

Murphy tried to answer. Waste of time. He struggled to keep his eyes open. The sack of shit knew he'd brought this on himself. *And yours truly has no problem giving it to you.* His cock twitched playfully in his jocks, appreciating the foreplay.

"Love to stay and chat, but I hear my mother calling." Baxter snickered and made sure Murphy saw him draw the knife from his boot before he placed the tip against his ear. He held him at arm's length and gauged how much ground the arterial spray would cover. A pantomime. One Murphy did not appreciate.

To hell with it. "It's been real, Murphy lad. Pity we can't do this again sometime." In one practiced swish of his blade, he sliced Murphy's throat from ear to ear, ducked, and listened to the son of a bitch's last breath drown in the blood pooling in his throat.

Served him right for screwing with the plan. He'd enjoy showing Sam, Jenna, everyone what it cost to mess with him. If time allowed, he'd have taken more of it to kill Murphy, but he had to find those fucking drugs. He owed for them big time, and Ugly Joe got off on breathing down his neck.

Sam denied it, but she must have found his stash and kept it for herself. She needed his money. The kennels were collapsing around her ears.

He'd considered doing her a favour, dousing the walls with petrol, when she took her softie break in Scarborough, but he'd gotten called for a meet with Ugly Joe and you never said no. Fire had always been a favourite. The toss of a lighted match, thorough, blistering heat, obliterated better than any knife or gun.

He covered Murphy with the tarp and piled a haybale on top of him. Jenna never came near the shed. Too many memories of her husband. *Who the fuck made wooden toys for a living?* He'd be long gone before they found the body. He picked up the bag of doggy treats and closed the door. One last rattle of the paddock before he strolled to his car. "Eenie-Meenie-Minie-Moe. Which of you losers is the first to go?"

CHAPTER EIGHTEEN

Perhaps the challenge in his voice did it, or the edge in his tone, but Sam's mouth went dry at Snake's order. Her heartbeat jumped. Game on, she lifted her chin. Their height difference meant nothing when their eyes met. The connection electric.

Who cared? She lifted the hem of her T-shirt, tugged it over her head, and didn't stop there. She shoved her jeans over her hips, kicked them aside, and faced him in only her underwear.

Snake didn't move. The heat of his gaze roamed lazily over her body before latching onto her lips.

"All of it," he murmured.

"At ease, soldier. What's your rush?" Cool morning air whispered over her skin. Goosebumps erupted on the back of her neck. They'd better hurry up unless Snake got off on kissing a woman who resembled an uncooked chicken.

Nervous fingers trembled over the hooks on Sam's bra. She hated to disappoint, but what if Snake preferred women with bigger breasts? All this angst for a kiss. Better be worth it. *Be sure.* Light from the fire blazed in Snake's light blue eyes as he watched her slide her underwear over her hips, snare the lace waistband with her big toe, and flick them onto the floor.

"Fuck me," he groaned.

"That's better. I thought you'd fallen asleep," she said and smiled.

"Nope. Wide awake." He caught her chin between his thumb and forefinger.

Her gaze drifted to his crotch, where the long ridge of his cock pressed against the denim of his jeans. "Mmm." She licked her lips, willed him to stay focused on his mission. The kiss.

"Come closer." His voice, always deep, plummeted to another level. Darker. Seductive.

Sam leaned into his space. One more step and she'd walk right into his skin. Lips pursed, she blew gently on his chin. "Your turn. Take off your shirt."

"Please?"

"Pretty please."

Steady fingers unbuttoned his shirt and there they were, well-toned pecs finally bared. A smattering of dark hair arrowed over his ripped abs and disappeared into his jeans.

"Turn around. Please." The tip of her pinkie on his shoulder encouraged the move. Damn hard work keeping the tremor out of her voice, her expression cool.

Above his broad back, a line of hair, cut military straight, graced the base of his skull. Tapered waist, solid hips, and an ass screaming for attention. Hell, yeah, he was beautiful.

Her tingling palm hovered in the space between his shoulder blades. When her gasp hit his neck, he flinched, but his hands stayed by his side. Silent permission for her to roam where she wished. Closer to sniff his lightly tanned skin. Her fingers trembled, ached to dig into his musky warmth. Mark him. Obliterate his stiff control. A gentle push on the base of his skull and his head bowed.

"Sam." Snake tried to turn, cursed when she stopped him.

"Shh." Relishing every stroke until they kissed, she began with the tip of her tongue exploring his velvety ear lobe. A quick nip and he gasped, spun to face her, and thrust his knee between her thighs.

Not willing to share her smile. Not yet. Sam pressed her lips together. And then it began. Dirty talk, sexy words, proven, practiced, fervent promises to make her wet.

Mouth hovering over his, she slipped her hand between his thighs. And pulled on the zipper. "Your pants are in the way."

"Happy to take them off? Just what kind of kissing did you have in mind?"

"Haven't decided. Right now, I'm enjoying watching your cock try its best to escape."

"Fine. Whatever you want."

He covered her hand with his, encouraging her to stroke harder. Blood pulsed in her ears, needing to taste. She was ready for a taste. Heady, like honey. A sharp, short thrust sent her hips crashing against his pelvis. Desire flared in his eyes. His jaw tightened.

"Tell me what you want, John." Simple words, not as graphic as his promises, but the flare of his nostrils said she'd hit her mark.

His gaze strayed briefly to her breasts before zeroing in on her mouth. Close, so close to that first kiss. She gasped, stifled a laugh when his hands grabbed her waist, and his hips gyrated hard against her, setting her core on fire.

It had been a long time since she had enjoyed the heat of a man. Not since Ed, and foreplay with him never carried this kind of burn.

"I want," he said, reminding her of her question. "To kiss every inch of you. Your lips, your breasts." He swept his hand between her legs. "Here. Until you come in my mouth screaming my name," he hissed.

His tongue ran across the seam of her lips and she gave his chest a gentle push.

Snake's head cocked to the side. "Too much? Want me to stop?"

As if. "No. You?"

In answer, his grip on her waist tightened. His tongue returned to her lips, seeking entry. *Why not?*

Sam cupped his arse, enjoyed the muscles flexing under her fingers, the way his cock pressed firmly against the front of her pelvis.

"You have an awesome arse," she noted. "Firm, perfect for filling out a pair of jeans." She reached forward. "An impressive cock."

"And you are a tease, Sam. Christ, what you do to me? Please, let me kiss you."

Sucking in a breath, she opened her mouth, allowed the tips of their tongues to touch, test. Eyes fixed on him, she stroked his pecs. Under her fingers, his heart beat strongly.

His nipple grew taut, and the muscles covering his rock-solid abdomen clenched. "About that kiss." His eyelids flickered.

She stroked the hard edge of his jaw and immediately regretted the loss of Snake's body heat even if the look in his eyes more than made up for it. A fucking vow loaded with a power that coursed from her toes to the crown of her head. An oath she shouldn't let him keep. "Is your kiss as amazing as you promised?" she asked, unsure she'd survive this man's undivided attention.

"Try me."

Hands glued to her hips, he pulled her closer. His gaze brushed over her lips, travelled to her breasts, and Sam swore self-combustion was not a myth.

"Please." Beads of sweat popped on her forehead and between her breasts.

Deep lines furrowed his brow as he tried hard not to push, to restrain his physical advantage and let her dictate the pace. This time, his silent plea melted the edges of her heart. She slid her hand around his cock and closed her fingers around his length. His erection pulsed against her palm. Her fingers found his balls. Easing and tightening, she caressed them until his breath hitched and his moan hummed in her ear.

"Sam... for fuck's sake," he begged, his head lifting to meet her gaze.

Snake's balls rested in her palm. "Don't move." Rising onto her toes, she sucked his bottom lip.

He shuddered, the pain of control deepening the line on his forehead, but he made no move to take the lead. "Tell me again, what do you want?" she asked, her breath shaky.

"To fuck you senseless, so for the love of God, kiss me and let's move on."

He moved swiftly, so fast she didn't have a chance to retreat, dived for her mouth and nipped her bottom lip. Again, harder this time, forcing her mouth to open and let him in. Mirroring the rhythm of her hand pumping his cock, he sucked on her tongue.

Without warning, her breath left her. An intense orgasm shuddering through her, seizing the air from her lungs.

"That's it. I've got you," he murmured. "Fucking amazing. I'm so damn hard for you."

She wanted to run, to pretend the last fifteen minutes hadn't happened. After the way she had led Ed to his death, she didn't deserve a second of the happiness she feared Snake could bring to her life.

He blew out a long breath and looked down at her, a question in his eyes. An answer she couldn't give, not now. Waiting, he arched an eyebrow. *Too much.* She turned her cheek and brushed it against his shoulder.

"Shh," she said, even though he hadn't said a word. "Time for bed."

"Lead on." Snake peppered kisses over her throat, and she swallowed a groan.

"Alone."

The smell of damp moss on the Yorkshire moor filtered through the half-open doorway.

CHAPTER NINETEEN

Sam took a sip and did her best not to spit the bitter sludge calling itself coffee into her mug. She may have spent last night alone in her room, but ghosts crowded her bed. Any way she turned, left, right or upside down, Ed stared her in the face.

The little hope she had that Snake would be long gone this morning went the same way as every other half-wish when it came to John. And as for his first name popping into her mind? Way too intimate.

Neither of them said a word, the kitchen dormant except for the crunch of toast devoured with the ferocity of two stags, locking horns over who got the girl.

Snake nudged the plate of bread towards her, offering the last slice. She shook her head, faked another sip of coffee, and drew her shoulders away from her ears. Time to bring the elephant into the room and see it on its way. "We need to talk."

"There's nothing to talk about."

Wow. Never would have picked Snake for a man who avoided confrontation. "So there's no confusion. We need to clear the air. As you said, we don't want things to get complicated."

Snake leaned back in his chair and fixed his gaze on the cup of coffee she waved in front of him. A muscle ticked in his jaw.

"I agreed to a kiss. Don't tell me you've changed your mind and want more. I'm not looking for commitment." His clipped tone irked.

The bang of her mug on the table brought his gaze straight to hers. "Don't worry, Snake. I, er… kiss lots of men." It hurt, more than she expected, that he found her this easy to dismiss.

Elbows resting on the table, his gaze boring into her, ice man nursed his coffee. Did he even guess that one shove of her knee under the table and he'd wear the disgusting stuff? Childish? Sure. Did it matter in her current mood? No.

Snake might have left active duty, but he hadn't lost the ability to compartmentalise. Well, neither had she. Fantastic kisser. Tick. Liked the way he let her take the lead. Tick. Enjoyed surrendering when he took control of the kiss. Two heavy black lines crossed in her mind. But if he could walk away, Sam could, too.

"Okay, then. No need to discuss it," he said.

Damn. Didn't even get the chance to toss her hair over her shoulder and huff. Confused by the mishmash of emotions swirling in her head, she missed the signal, didn't prepare. Snake moved with that spooky speed of his and grabbed her hand.

"Agree. Nothing to discuss." Her voice shook. "When are you leaving?" She twisted from his grip.

"After lunch. I'll help you muck out the kennels first."

"No need. Jim can do that." Her breath hitched. "I'm going to have a shower. I probably won't see you before you go—drive safely."

Blowing out a breath, Snake crossed to the window and drew the curtain aside. The smell of damp moss on the moor filtered through the narrow opening at the top. He narrowed his eyes against the glare of the sun and listened to the water pounding in the shower. The two he'd already had this morning did nothing to calm his horny cock or erase the memory of Sam's hands on his body. Her lips.

Ready to hit the road, he shrugged on his leather jacket and tried his fucking hardest to walk to the door. Almost made it. Then he heard her singing.

Unlike his toneless one note croaks in the shower, Sam had a fantastic voice. No sodding surprise. The woman oozed talent from every provocative pore of her body. Why not add another to the growing list?

His forehead banged softly on the door. What he wouldn't give to be standing next to her, caressing her breasts. His soapy fingers gliding over her slender thighs, stroking her flat abdomen, pinching and rolling her nipples between his fingers. Cupping her perfectly round arse and sliding his fingers into her. Sweat beaded on his brow.

She asked him what he wanted. To make love to you, is what he should have said. Honest, no room for guessing. He'd settled for a kiss. And one kiss would never be enough. Not with Sam. He craved her more than his next meal.

One fist raised, ready to knock, show her a proper goodbye, a see ya she'd never forget. *Walk away.*He didn't want to leave, but if she invited him to stay, he'd demand more. And she showed no interest in treading that path. That had to make two of them. Wedded to locating Seckou, his team counted on him to stay sharp. Not get distracted by a kiss from a woman who confounded the hell out of him. Head finally in gear, his feet hit the steps.

CHAPTER TWENTY

Snake's knuckles hovered over the closed metal door of the boss' office. Before he knocked, out of habit he checked in with the security camera to his right. When they transferred the Sentinel operation from Knight's Chalk Farm to their new HQ, he'd taken pride in sourcing and setting up the state-of-the-art security system. An image of the non-functional cameras he'd noticed at Sam's flashed in his mind. He made a mental note to do something about them the next time he was at the kennels. With twats like Baxter hanging around, she couldn't be too careful.

After all, everyone trusted their comms man to have surveillance under control. But it didn't matter how often he reminded himself of the value he brought to the Sentinel. The same questions played in his mind. Had he fully earned the right to be there, earned his spot on the team? Did he belong?

Entirely his shit. No one hinted it might be the case. But Knight, Doc, and Spanner would always be the three musketeers who tolerated him. The man who stepped in when Mike died, but who could never take his place.

He shouldn't care this much. No one fully walked in another person's shoes, but to the foster kid, always on the outside when it came to family, belonging went way past a chin lift when he walked in the room. It was everything.

"Come in," Knight's voice boomed.

Spanner slapped his shoulder as soon as he entered. "How's Sam's ankle? Been giving it plenty of massages?" he asked, holding a tray of sandwiches, his trademark celebrity smile plastered all over his smug face.

Snake must have missed the message that said this was a team meeting. He flashed Spanner a shut-the-fuck-up glare and faked a punch to blondie's gut.

"Ow. Just a question, mate. Catcha." Spanner thrust the tray of sandwiches at Snake's chest.

He assumed the meeting had been called to discuss his latest intel from Mali, but as no one else had arrived, perhaps not.

Knight nodded at the chair in closest to his desk. The reclaimed wooden slab, supported by heavy-duty, extra thick steel, looked innocent until you pressed a few buttons. Snake preferred the chair slightly left of centre, and not knowing where else to put the tray, he perched it on the seat next to him, stretched his legs in front of him, and waited for Knight to finish writing.

A bank of monitors lined one wall. At one end was the locked reinforced steel door leading to the weapons' safe. At the other end, the kitchen. A fucking chef's paradise, mainly there for Spanner's benefit, their self-appointed chef.

He'd never noticed it before, but today the clock on the shelf behind the boss caught his eye. Damn mobile phones had taken over many jobs, including telling the time. loud ticking reported every nervous second as he tried to figure out why Knight had summoned him.

Daily workouts were a must, a morning ritual when they weren't on a mission, but since he returned from Sam's, Knight hadn't stuck around for the breakfast that usually followed. Snake assumed he'd been neck deep in finalising details for Sentinel's new operation in New York.

The clock kept ticking. Snake drew in an audible breath, straightened his spine, and eyeballed the tray of sandwiches. "So, boss, how is it going in New York? When do we open?" He shoved his hands in his pockets and leaned back in his chair, expecting Knight to play the long game.

No mucking around. The boss' steely gaze hit him square on. "I'm glad you asked."

"You are? Problems?"

Knight scratched the edge of his mouth with his index finger. "No."

Fucking torture. Irritated by the closed answer to what he thought was an invitation, Snake smoothed his sweaty palms over his pants and tried not to let his frustration take hold. "You said you wanted to see me, boss. What's up?"

"I did. Thanks for coming on such short notice."

couldn't help it. Still expecting the rest of the team to join them any second, he glanced over his shoulder. When the door stayed shut, he cleared his throat. "Sure, boss. What can I do for you?"

"I have a proposition for you."

Interesting. Tic toc. His heart caught up with the clock. His brain forming any excuse not to return to Sam's place even if he was missing his damn dog.

"Would you be interested in leading the New York team?"

Snake almost choked. His coughing drowning the clock's commentary as time froze. "Me? With Spanner?"

Knight chuckled and poured a glass of water from the jug on his desk. "Here. No. Spanner has his hands full."

A nip of the hard stuff sitting on the credenza behind the boss would have gone down more easily, but he took what Knight offered and cocked his head to the side. There had to be more.

"We will need a longer conversation to work out the details, and I realise you might need some time to think about it before you decide, but don't take too long. If you accept, I expect you to be ready to leave soon. Over the next few months, they'll complete the structural work on the facilities, but you'll have to bring it up to an operational standard."

"Will I have a say in the team?" He had to ask. If choosing his personnel wasn't on the table, there'd be no more discussion.

"Wouldn't have it any other way. If you accept, you can give me your suggestions, and we'll work it out to our mutual satisfaction, but I don't anticipate any problems. You okay with that?"

"Sure. Thanks, boss. For considering me. It's big. I'll give you my answer soon."

"Good man. And Snake, let me be clear, you were my first choice. I trust you to do the job, but if it's not what you're looking for, I can find someone else."

"Understood. That it, boss?" Heart pounding, he levered himself out of the chair and strode to the door.

"Not quite."

One heartbeat too many dropped straight to his boots. *Here it comes.* Too focused on the backhander, he didn't anticipate the throat punch.

"Hope you've got nothing planned for a few hours. We're meeting Sam at the café."

Hearing Sam's name stirred that part of him that didn't appreciate being disturbed. "Sorry, boss, I said I'd catch up with Doc to—"

Knight waved his hand in the air. "Message Doc, tell him you're busy. Sam's got a problem, and I promised Lily we'd take care of it. You two were getting on well at the party. I assumed you'd be happy to help."

Again, with the Cheshire Cat grin. *Take note, practice for the new job.* "Sure, boss. Sam's good people."

"Especially her smart mouth, right?"

121

Snake nodded. He more than liked her mouth. Spent too much fucking time dreaming of ways she could use it to bring him more pleasure than he'd ever known. "Yeah." They exchanged mutual nods and commiserating shoulder shrugs.

"Let's go." Knight tossed him the keys to the SUV. "You drive. I know how you hate being late."

CHAPTER TWENTY-ONE

Whatever had possessed her to call Lily? Not too deep in her subconscious, she knew the conversation would mobilise the mighty forces of Sentinel into action. *Whoop-de-doo*. Sam twirled her finger in the air and stared through the window at the sky.

Early afternoon, and winter's gloom shrouded London city, the air bone-deep damp. Sam had avoided any major stuff-ups on the way down, but if she hoped to reach the kennels before snow slowed traffic on the motorway to a complete standstill, it would not happen. Not if she spent another fifteen minutes circling the block, working up the courage to face Knight.

Built into the front of the tube station, the small café was famous for toasted baps and knock-the-back-of-your-head-off coffee, her friends claimed it as a favourite haunt.

Anyhow, if the cosmos, growing gloomier by the second, had a sliver of compassion, Knight should have gotten fed up waiting by now and been long gone. Sam sank her nose below the edge of her thick, woolly scarf, hauled her body out of the car, and surrendered.

No use wimping out now, and as if the cosmos agreed, immediately when she turned the corner, Lily's man locked her in his sights.

He sat at a table by the window, looking more like Alfie the Alligator than the CEO of a clandestine security company. His unblinking, steely grey eyes bored into her.

A bell tinkled over the door. When she entered, she immediately recognised Snake. He must have heard her come in, but he kept his back to her, frustration rolling off the wall of stubborn muscle. *Don't forget. Cranky when late.* It had been a few weeks, but the pleasure of his kiss lingered like her favourite ice-cream on her lips.

Pity a future didn't exist that included a Sam and Snake story. *Danger.* The kick in her heart rate warned of the potential disaster. The logical outcome if they had taken things further and shared wounds over dinner and dessert.

Unfortunately, the lunch crowd had been and gone. No munching strangers to break the tension, distract from her lopsided footsteps limping towards them.

Knight waved her over to where their knees poked out either side of the small table, swamped by their size. Snake persisted, didn't look at her until she levelled with the table.

A library of unsaid thoughts hid behind his translucent blue eyes. The tips of her ears prickled. The meeting held all the suspense of a dentist visit rather than coffee with friends.

"Glad you made it." Knight toed the leg of a bright yellow metal chair in her direction. His reflexes kicked in, catching it before it fell.

"Sam." Snake sniffed and shoved a menu in front of her.

His eyes did that thing, the head-to-toe body scan, the roll of his full lips. *Too skinny, no tits?* She couldn't resist returning his eyeball flick. "Snake." Keep up the single word sentences and it would be Christmas before she asked for Sentinel's help.

"Can I get you a coffee?" Knight asked, glancing at the door. "Are you on your own?"

"Yes, I am, and no to coffee. Thanks." Refusing desperately needed caffeine felt bizarrely like being in control. *Pathetic.* "I can't stay long. Must get home. Time for a quick chat, then…"

"Is that what we're calling it?" Snake murmured.

His scowl hit with back-handed relief. The perfect out—escape. "Look, sorry. This is a mistake." She stood quickly, keen for a quick exit.

"Snake, shut the fuck up." Knight rattled her empty seat. "Sam, sit. Please." Lily's Mr Cool clasped his hands and rested them on the table.

Accept the offer. Her ankle screamed. Careful to keep her bum close to the edge of the seat, a getaway plan percolating, she did as he asked.

Knight huffed. "Let me get you that coffee."

"Thanks. I'd prefer tea."

"Tea it is. Kids, behave. I'll be right back."

Alone with Snake, her left pinkie fluttered, ached for physical contact, to touch the steel-grey T-shirt visible under Snake's black biker jacket. Unlike her, he never hinted at feeling cold.

"How's the ankle?" Snake's nose tipped nose at her leg.

"No problem. See?" She circled her foot, the move causing the chair to rock on three legs. An audible gasp flew from her lips.

Before she could blink, Snake caught her elbow and stopped her from falling.

"Here, switch with me." He shifted sideways.

"Thanks." She dismissed the temptation to ask, show interest in what he'd been doing lately. After he'd left the kennels, she considered their one-night contract completed. Nice while it lasted.

Any excuse not to look at him. She offered a dog update. "George is doing well." Her clipped tone intentionally implying he'd forgotten to ask.

"Good to know. I planned on visiting in the next couple of weeks. That's if you don't mind?"

No. No visits. "Sure, he'll be pleased to see you." Laugh. In a perfect world, her mouth might sync with her brain.

"Bounce okay? She's not with you?"

"No. At home, with Jim."

"That ankle looks as though it's still giving you trouble. Had it X-rayed yet?"

"No need. Tom will be glad to see you. He keeps asking when you're coming for a rematch." He didn't answer and they fell into a clumsy silence until Knight returned took a sip of his coffee, and finally the time had come.

"How can we help, Sam? Lily said you sounded concerned when you rang," Knight said.

"Someone is trying to kill my dogs." This time, her mouth rocketed ahead of her brain. Words bouncing off the tiled walls before she stopped them.

Knight cleared his throat. Snake growled. "Don't worry, Snake. George is fine."

"I'm not worried about my fucking dog."

Sam swallowed. Whenever they spent time together, things had a habit of shooting from zero to one hundred in less than ten seconds.

"And?" Knight ignored them.

"The evening before last, I went out to feed them before heading to bed. It was dark. I could have imagined it, but I thought I saw someone hanging out around the training shed. It might have been the man… you remember, Snake?"

"Baxter. That son of a bitch." Snake threw his clenched fists onto the table.

"Jesus, man. Stand down. Carry on, Sam. Take your time. Who's Baxter?" Knight patted her hand, which did weird shit to her insides.

Another sip of tea slowed her pulse. The tension around the table matched the pent-up energy in her closed fists. "Hero here saw a man on my property. Uninvited, but I reckoned he must have been curious, come to check the place out. People do that sometimes, arrive without an appointment."

"And who's Baxter?" Knight repeated

"He used to work for me until I fired him for mistreating my dogs." It pissed her off that she couldn't be sure because then she wouldn't need to be here asking for help, sitting so close to Snake. But, for Jenna's sake, she couldn't accuse him, not without proof.

"Which shed?" Snake asked, less successful than Knight at hiding his irritation.

"Over by where we moved the silos. It's possible I am overreacting, trying to connect dots that don't exist." A collective groan circled the table. "But that night, three of the dogs got sick. They're still at the vet."

"George?" Snake asked, a deep swallow visibly shifting the lump in his throat.

"No. As I said, he's okay." Under the table, her fingers ached to reach out, reassure him, but she didn't go for mixed messages.

"Bounce?"

"Yes. She's never far from my side, but I'd forgotten George's marrow bones. They were in the fridge. I ordered her to stay with the others while I went back to the house. I…"

Tears pricked the corner of her eye. Snake seized her hand. This time, she didn't fight. His strong fingers wrapped around her fingers, his thumb stroking the inside of her wrist anchored her.

"Did you call the police?" Knight asked.

"No. I'm sure they have better things to do with their time, plus I didn't want to risk adding two and two and coming up with six."

"Now you've had time to consider. What's your gut tell you?"

"That I must have fucked up, missed the expiry date on their food."

"Bollocks." Snake let go of her hand.

Feeling as though she'd been tossed from a plane, her body tensed. "Could be. I have to find out for sure what's going on and I thought maybe Sentinel might help. It's not your usual type of assignment, but if anything happened to my dogs because I missed something vital, I'd… well, that's why I called you. I wondered if maybe you'd send someone to look around."

"Of course. Snake will return with you. He's familiar with the place. You can show him where it happened, and he'll do a preliminary recon. After he reports, we'll take it from there."

Feeling stupid, helpless. She fucking hated it, the way this situation harpooned her to Afghanistan and the greatest balls up of her life.

"Don't worry, Sam," Knight reassured. "Until we have this sorted, we'll stick with you. Now drink your tea. Want something to eat? They serve mean looking pastries. Lily can't resist them."

Whenever he said his wife's name, all Knight's hard edges softened.

"No thanks, I had a late lunch."

"Talking of sweet teeth. Look who's walked through the door."

Sam noted the surprise in Knight's voice as Crystal pushed past the waitress offering her a menu and rushed over to meet them. Her mass of blonde curls poked in odd directions, as though she'd tumbled out of bed in a hurry.

"What's up, Crystal? Looking for Lily? She's home." Knight nodded over his shoulder toward their flat. "I'm going back now. She ordered pastries. What can I get you?"

"No, nothing." Crystal swayed.

Need more coffee, or a late night? Crystal and Spanner often hit the clubs when he flew home from a job.

"Knight. I'm sorry to interrupt, but can we talk? Alone, please."

"Sure. Welcome to my office. He swept his hand over the table."

Snake and Sam shared a curious glance, but she wasn't about to stick her nose in where it didn't belong. Plus, she'd already taken up too much of the boss' time. "Here, Crystal, have my seat." Sam offered. "We're leaving. Thanks, Knight. I'll be in touch."

Crystal half-smiled, pecked her on the cheek, and collapsed into the empty chair.

Snake stood too, placed his palm on the small of her back, and guided her to the exit. "My ride's over there, the Jeep. Follow me to my place. It's not far, won't take me a minute to grab an overnight bag and we're on our way."

"Thanks. I'm sure I'm overreacting. Maybe you should…"

The tip of Snake's fingers grazed her lips.

"Shh. We're wasting time. Snow's coming down hard."

CHAPTER TWENTY-TWO

Sam glanced in her rear-view mirror at Snake, who drove a safe distance behind her. The grey curtain of snow softened the edges of his SUV but did nothing to dim the intensity of his eyes burning holes into the back of her neck.

An upfront girl, used to stating her mind and moving on, she wasn't comfortable with her pent up anger. Not knowing where to channel her frustration made her nervous. One bloody kiss and the Snake acted like she'd left him at the altar, and last check, he'd left without saying goodbye.

A bloody long day. Her fingers drummed the steering wheel. Music would be welcome if the car radio could fix on a station. Flashes of old Sam, the woman who took care of herself, met everyone on the same level, nagged all the way up the motorway. Chuck them in with a healthy dose of guilt for bothering Sentinel in the first place and she itched for a fight or a fuck. Anything to take the pressure down.

And of all the men on the planet, why did Knight have to pick Snake to check her place? Surely he had someone else. His teams couldn't all be saving the world. She slammed her boot onto the accelerator. Tyres screeching, the car zigzagged across the snow. The dumb act of unwarranted defiance earned three justified toots from Snake. "What's the matter, soldier? Can't handle a little speed?" She raised her middle finger over her head.

Unfortunately, goading Snake didn't stop the toing and froing in her gut. Her better half dreamt of the long, hot bubble bath she planned to sink into as soon as she touched home base. According to Lily, a dash of the lavender oil she'd left behind should tease out the aches from her body and stop her skull from throbbing.

Sam leaned slightly and snatched her water bottle off the floor by her feet. Often, she loved driving at this time of day, when the sun clung to the horizon, scattering burnt orange light over the road to the house. No chance this evening. Snow fell from the blue-grey clouds and danced like manic fairies in the glow of the headlights.

Warmth from the heater finally found her bones as the barn came into sight. Her eyelids drooped as the vehicle swerved to a sudden stop in front of the house. Snake roared in behind, climbed out of his Jeep, and prowled with the grace of a snow leopard towards her.

Eyes fixed on his prey, legs, torso, and arms shifting in perfect unison, Snake claimed the space between them. The most impressive looking man she'd ever laid eyes on never failed to make her toes curl. Striking, although she couldn't put her finger on a single part of his anatomy that highlighted the point.

In the military, she'd hung out with many tall, in-shape men. Muscles built on muscles. While soldiers waited for action, they stayed busy working out and cleaning their weapons. From memory, none of them swaggered with Snake's confidence. Plain as the nose on his perfect face, he didn't have to bench press above his weight to prove his competence in all things physical.

Sam closed her eyes, steadied herself, and willed the heat rising in her blood to chill, her heart rate to slow. When they'd kissed, his body felt hard, powerful, but somehow in need of a hug. *Christ*. Where the hell did her mind intend going with this? Nowhere complicated. She settled her gaze on the scar slicing across his pec. New, raw.

Her face flushed, and a growl rumbled in her throat, as she thought of a million ways she'd enjoy kissing the scowl off his face. Her smile at this fantasy swiftly evaporated. *Jim!* Damn, she'd forgotten inviting him to dinner.

"Open the door. You're getting cold," Snake muttered through the snow sticking to the stubble on his chin.

With the hood of his jacket pulled up over his head, he doubled as a growly Father Christmas. "Patience," she said.

"What you looking at?" Snake's gaze locked on her lips.

"Your ugly mug. Hang on a sec while I tell Jim we're here."

"Who's Jim?"

He must have forgotten their earlier conversation, and the hint of jealousy in his voice made her feel shabby, guilty. Aside from being a bitch, she should find a less energy-intensive way of keeping Snake at arm's length.

She opened her door, planted her weight onto her uninjured foot, hobbled to the front of the car, and leaned on the bonnet. Her head now thumped in time to Jim's shit taste in music blaring from the speakers rocking her house. Forget Jim. Forget dinner. How quickly could she get Snake set up in the barn before she made it to bath and bed?

She needed sleep, lots of sleep. "Make your way to the barn and I'll be with you in a tick." The mobile connection had been intermittent on the motorway, most likely because of the bad weather, and she still had to talk with the vet. Fingers crossed her dogs were better and could come home tomorrow.

Inside the house, Jim looked as knackered as she felt. Perfectly happy to call it an early night when she promised to make it up to him tomorrow and cook Shepherd's Pie.

That's one way to keep warm. Snake stood outside the barn, chucking snowballs at the barn wall. An opportunity too good to miss. She packed together one of her own. "Duck!" Too late. The missile hit his head and dissolved into a squelchy mess.

"Oh. You are dead, sweetheart." Chin tucked to his chest, his pale eyes sparkling, Snake charged.

The slippery ground and her bung ankle made it impossible to run. Too easily, one hand grabbed her elbow, the other caught her behind her knees, and he hoisted her onto his shoulder.

"Let me go. You're hurting me." Head dangling next to his backside, her laugh should have betrayed her lie.

"Sorry." Snake set her on her feet and shifted away.

"Er. No problem. Believe me. I'm okay," she assured him, shaking her head, as she fiddled with the rusty padlock securing the barndoor. "I'm not sure what you hope to find in here." Her heart, for starters, as it left her body any time he got close.

A groan and a push and the double wooden doors swung open. With no windows, the long, rectangular building acted like a train tunnel. Too dark to see much, even after they turned on the heavy-duty torches hanging from the wall. Sam sighed. "Sorry, looks like I've wasted your time."

"Never. Tomorrow, after you're rested and there's more light, we can try again. Why don't we go up to the house? You must be hungry. I can meet Jim and you can fill me in what's been happening. Shall we?"

Snake's palm on her shoulder sent shivers that had nothing to do with the icicles clinging to the barn door running along her spine.

Sam shrugged, releasing herself from his touch. "Jim's leaving. I asked him to join us for dinner tomorrow night. I'm happy to make you coffee, or there's beer left over from Lily's party, but I have a date with a hot bath and bed."

Snake stopped mid-stride and faced her. She would have loved hearing why, but Jim opened the front door and George flew out of the house. Tail wagging ferociously, he slobbered his master with wet kisses.

"Hey, boy. How are you?" Large hands cupped the dog's face. "I've missed you," he whispered, his nose disappearing into the fur on the top of George's head. "I see he made it into the house."

Snake winked and Sam's body temperature shot from normal to well overheated. "Sometimes. Special privileges. The perks of his new job."

"Job?"

Sam bit her bottom lip. She'd meant to give Snake a call and fill him in sooner but hadn't found the right moment to bother the man. "Tom's been taking him to the hospital when Jenna's on shift. Turns out George has a way with her patients. He's become quite a celebrity with some of the military vets she treats."

"Hey, Sam. I've left you soup on the stove," Jim interrupted, a slow smile creeping over his lips.

"Thanks." She pecked him on the cheek. "Thanks for looking after me."

"Always. See you tomorrow for that pie." He winked and exchanged nods with Snake. "Evening."

"Look forward to it. Enjoy your evening, Jim. Snake, go on in. You and George have a lot of catching up to do, and I need a bath. First, I'll check on Meadow and the pups."

"I can come with," he offered.

"No thanks. The more I think about it, the more I'm convinced I brought you here on a wild goose chase. Any human error is entirely down to me."

Sam sat on the veranda, rocking gently in the old wicker chair. As much as she'd been looking forward to soaking in her bath, surrounded by candles, Lily's smells, and a very welcome glass of Chablis, climbing the stairs to her bedroom ranked as a major stumbling block. The warmth from the small heater thawed her toes, and, she suspected, gave her a very attractive Rudolph nose.

Sitting in her much-loved granny chair, neck pressed against the faded embroidered cushion, the end of her nose traced the path of a moth fluttering in and out of the thick beams. Same as ninety-five percent of the old farmhouse, the roof needed fixing. During winter, the house fires kept the dry rot away, but come spring, if one of her grant applications didn't come through, the place might collapse.

Tomorrow she'd arranged for assessors from a major charity to visit. Fingers crossed that they'd give the tick to her set-up and make a sizeable donation to the Mates for Mates program. She hadn't finished sharing the news with Snake, but she should. After all, George deserved credit for the new idea of training dogs as companions for military vets with PTSD. She'd been reading up on the many ways they could help. Anything from signalling an episode or reminding a person to take medication. Fascinating.

Big cheers to that. Encouraged by the toe of her boot, the chair rocked in a soothing rhythm. Red wine sloshed in the glass resting in her lap. "What do you think? Is it possible for a person to be more than bone tired?" she asked the moth, who'd found a friend. "Tendon tired? Sinew sleepy?" she slurred, adding a snort, as if that made a point. Not very attractive. Good job Snake had gone to bed. No witnesses.

Instead of making it easier, the grog made it harder to shift her arse and take that first step to bed. Each sip dragged her deeper into self-doubt. Convinced her calling Lily about the dogs had been a dumb idea. She'd allowed the shit with Baxter to get the better of her, unnerve her to the point of paranoia.

In the morning, when Snake inevitably found no evidence, she'd apologise for dragging him all the way up north for nothing and watch him walk away for a second time. If she had paid more attention to the butcher bones, checked they were fit to eat, she might not be contemplating another drink, wishing she'd saved Snake a trip.

Bounce shuffled beside her and lifted her face for a chin scrub. Tears threatened. "If anything happened to you, girl..." George joined for a sniff and blink. Their empathic whining chased the dark out of the night, challenged the moon. Dogs spoke fluent lonely.

"Okay, okay." Placing her hands on the arms of the rickety rocker, she gave a push, failed to make it to her feet, and flopped onto the chair. Well and truly beached, Sam lost it. A spray of red wine shot from her mouth. Unable to move, she must look like the doomed victim in a bad horror movie. Stuck outside on a snowy night, with no one to hear her cries.

Bounce shuffled her backside on the wood floor and rested her chin on Sam's lap. "I'm trying, sweetheart. Give me a minute. And yes. You can sleep with me tonight. Both of you," she reassured George, who frantically wagged his tail. "But shh, don't tell anyone." The finger aimed at her lips missed and poked her nose. "Okay, one, two, three." Exhaling loudly this time, she made it to her feet and wobbled into the house.

In winter, her bedroom doubled as an ice cave. *Sod the bath, you'll probably drown.* Too tired, more than a little tipsy, she had no hope. She kicked off her boots and face-planted into the bed.

The dogs snuck as close to the bed as they dared without jumping up to join her and wagged their tails. "Good dogs. Up." With the quilt tucked snugly under her chin, her icy toes found a toasty spot under Bounce's backend.

When she'd looked in the mirror that morning, the crow's feet outlining her eyes meant she must have smiled in the past. Before. Not now. Buried under the heaviness in her chest lived stuff she didn't deserve. Happiness, pleasure.

Ed and Arash dying had robbed her of any chance of a positive future, leaving her mad at everything and anyone. *Forget the past.* If only. Blackness claimed her vision. Snake slept in the spare room. The hot, human body she'd prefer to be playing footsy with. Bounce huffed and rubbed his wet nose against her little toe.

CHAPTER TWENTY-THREE

One eye open, Sam jackknifed out of bed. *Fuck.* Bark, bark, scream. *Foxes!* Add electric fence to the growing list of must haves. She couldn't have been asleep for more than an hour. The bastards were after Meadow's pups.

Luckily, she hadn't undressed before collapsing, but where were her soddin' boots? No time to find where she'd kicked them off, so she shoved her feet into her slippers. They'd have to do.

Alarmed by her sudden departure from the bed, the dogs stood on the duvet, ears pricked.

"Stay." She held up her hand and closed the door, blocking them from following. She didn't want them taking off after the foxes.

She grabbed her parka from the peg on the front door, wrapped her scarf around her neck, and stepped outside into the sleet zigzagging across the yard. The light sensors hadn't activated. Pitch black except for the distinct green glow of fox eyes gleaming in the dark. Three. At least.

"Get out of here." Tails dropped, the arrogant shits backed away.

The smell of burning wood hit her with the force of ten tanks. *Oh no.* Down the path, smoke rose from the kennels. No wonder the buggers weren't game to come closer. The fire kept them at bay.

Ignoring her injured ankle, Sam belted towards the kennel and cursed. Now was not the time to be without boots. Damn slippers. Dumb move. Tongue pressed firmly against the roof of her mouth, she struggled to hold onto the breath tearing from her lungs. A loud crack to her left and a branch fell from a tree. Her foot slipped to the side, shooting daggers along her thigh.

Afraid the foxes might chance it and head for Meadow and the pups. "Shoo! Back off!" Sam waved her arms above her head, but the fuckers stood their ground, daring her to face the fire.

Smoke funnelled from the roof of the barn and hit the canopy of zig-zagging sleet. Tearing her scarf from her neck, she dunked it in the bucket of water by the door and held it to her mouth and nose. Not much protection from the fumes, but it might allow time to reach the pups.

Clouds of thick grey smoke billowed from the open barn door. She swiped her runny nose and clamped her scarf over her mouth. Tucking her chin against her chest, tried not to cough, and entered the barn. No matter which way she turned, flames licked the path. Seconds left to find Meadow and her pups and get the hell out of there before the roof collapsed and the entire building caved.

Gritting her teeth, she ignored the searing pain in her feet. Pathetic slippers were doing a naff job of protecting them. Just when she thought she'd have to abandon the rescue, she swore she heard a tiny voice. "Hello. Anyone there?" It was hard to make out any human sound above the roar of the fire.

"Over here. I can't get out."

Tom. Please no. Heart in her throat, she took a step forward. "Where are you?" Squinting, fingers brushing the sweat from her stinging eyes, she strained to see through the smoke. Sweet sod all moved.

"I'm stuck." Tom's croaky voice came from her left.

"Okay, hold on. I'm coming to..." A fit of coughing drowned the rest of her sentence. Black soot covered the outside of her scarf, but no way would she leave him. Sidestepping smoking debris, Sam kept moving. The face of the little girl in the hotel flashed in front of her. Her hands curled into tight fists. *Move.* They would not die because she couldn't get her head on straight.

"Hell. Sam? Are you in there?"

"Snake?" Her legs gave way. One hand shot out to stop herself from falling. Her fingers latched onto a white-hot hook. *Damn.* "Over here."

"Hang on."

Never happier to hear anyone's voice in her entire life. Sheer relief gave her the strength to claim what air remained in her lungs. "Hurry. Tom's trapped."

Snake pulled off his beanie and pressed it against Sam's scarf. "What the hell are you doing? We need to get out of here. Now."

"No. Tom's in here."

Fantastic.

Sam pushed past him. "Keep talking, Tom."

"I'm scared. I can't get out," Tom whimpered.

Every muscle in Snake's body shifted into operational mode. Sam looked ready to drop. He grabbed her elbow and spun her to face the exit. "I'll get Tom. Stay low. Leave." He gave her a push, grabbed the collar of his shirt, and pulled it over his nose and mouth.

"Fine. You get Tom. But I'm not leaving Meadow and the pups."

Chucking Sam over his shoulder crossed his mind. But experience said she'd argue, and they didn't have time for a fight. "Where are they?"

"With Tom."

"Triffic. Okay. Stay close."

Flames snapped and sizzled in an angry circle around Tom and the dogs. Slumped over Meadow, he shielded her and the pups with his body.

"Okay, mate. Time to get out of here." In one well-practiced movement, Snake hoisted the lad over his shoulder and turned for the exit.

"No. Let me go. Meadow? Sam, don't leave them," he moaned.

"Right behind you, Tom. I've got them."

Out of the corner of his eye, Snake glimpsed Sam scooping up the pups. Her chest heaved. Too much smoke.

"Meadow. Come." She whistled at the dog limping behind her.

Not for the first time in his life, Snake wished he had an extra pair of hands. Breathing in and out through his nose, he stumbled out of the barn, fell to his knees, and gently lowered Tom onto the ground. "Hey Tom, open your eyes." He gently slapped the lad's pale cheek. "You're okay. Stay here. I'm going to get Sam."

Coughing and retching, Tom rolled onto his side. Snake placed one hand firmly on the boy's heaving shoulder. "Hang in there. You'll be okay. I'll be right back."

Snake turned to the barn. Flames soared above it, spitting at the sky, and his heart somersaulted. Any minute, the roof could collapse. *No.* He couldn't lose Sam. Not like this.

Arms flying everywhere, Tom tried to sit. "I said. Don't move." The lad kept struggling. Snake raised his hand and contemplated knocking the kid out for his safety when Sam staggered from the haze carrying the pups, Meadow at her heels.

Tom wrestled from his grip. "Easy, they're okay." He tilted his head and thanked heave for the falling snow.

Sam fell against him, and the breath whooshed free of his lungs as he grabbed her waist and lowered her beside Tom. The pups spilled into the boy's arms, yipping and licking at his face.

Needing to reassure himself Sam was there and not burned to a crisp, he ran his hand over her body, checked for injuries, and brushed a strand of hair from her black face. Her eyes were blank, her gaze fixed on a spot behind him. Gently, he gripped her shoulders and gave them a shake. "Hey. You okay?"

"Y… es," she spluttered. "Fine. You?"

Way beyond happy to have her beside him, tears lodged in his throat. Too choked to speak, he nodded, convinced if anyone ever asked him, he fell in love with her that night.

"What the fuck happened?" Out of nowhere, carrying blankets, Jim waved a torch. "Fire and ambulance are on the way." Sirens blared in the distance.

Wide eyes fixed on the burning barn, Sam shuffled to her feet. Terrified she'd take off and try to save it, he wrapped his arms around her waist and pulled her to him. "Forget it, Sam. There's nothing you can do."

Her sobs tore through the night, ripping his heart from his chest. He peppered kisses over her forehead, lifted her chin, and willed her to look at him. "We can rebuild the barn, Sam. We're alive. That's the main thing. I'm sorry." A shit-stupid thing to say.

The ambulance pulled over a few feet away. "Come on, let's get you and Tom looked at before we can talk to the police." No question this was arson. Sam might object, but he planned on staying at the farm until they found out who lit the fire and why.

Sam shivered. Her small frame shuddered against him. Male or female, it didn't matter who you were. Life could bring the toughest to their knees. His palm cupped her cheek. "You're safe, sweetheart. No one's hurt." He stopped short of promising everything was okay.

"Why, Snake?" Sam's breath stuttered in the freezing air.

"Later. We'll find out. I promise. But you need to see a medic. Both of you." He nodded at Tom, who stood next to him, his arms wrapped tightly around his middle. Snake raised his hand in the air. "High five. Good job, Spitfire. You were amazing in there. Because of you, Meadow and her pups are alive."

Tom's palm slapped his. Snake's parents had died in a light plane crash before he started high school. Family life had given him a pass, but as he drew Tom in for a group hug, a strange sense of belonging washed over him.

"Where are the pups? Meadow?" Head on a swivel, Sam searched for the dogs.

Not knowing what else to do, he grabbed her hands and placed them over his heart. "Easy, they're here. Jim's taking care of them."

"Oh…" Sam's tears returned, and he wanted to draw her into his arms, but her flinch stopped him.

He understood. After a shit-show, if she felt remotely the same way he did, she needed space. "Bet you wish I had that handkerchief, right?"

Sam grimaced, but he told himself she meant to smile because, right now, her smile stopped him from crumbling.

"Everyone okay here?" A heavy bag slung over his shoulder; the paramedic headed straight for Tom.

Snake released the boy and gave him an encouraging shove. "Go on. Let him check you out. We're right here." He searched for somewhere for Sam to sit. Too late, he watched as her eyes rolled in her head and her legs crumpled under her. "Hell, sweetheart. Hold on."

CHAPTER TWENTY-FOUR

Baxter clung to the edge of the tree line, freezing his balls off, keen not to be seen, but he couldn't miss the entertainment. He swallowed the cheer threatening to erupt from his mouth and jerked harder on his cock.

Taking pleasure. Admiring one's work was important. An essential ingredient for his self-esteem. A quick peek from his hiding place confirmed no one bothered to look his way. Safe to take a step from behind the tree to enjoy every delightful second of the inferno. From the first strike of the match, the flames had gobbled everything in their path.

He slowed his hand, but kept up a steady rhythm, a controlled rise to climax. The fire raged, taller than any bonfire, a fucking beacon lighting up the night sky, mirroring his anger, cursing the loss of the cushy kennel job. The dogs never went anywhere near the silos. A perfect hiding place for his drugs. No chance of them sniffing out his stash, but never satisfied, Sam had moved the fucking things. Now he couldn't find them.

Turning her precious business to a pile of ash. *Serves you right, bitch.* Sure as shit, Sam deserved everything coming to her, payback for firing him. Why? Chaining Bounce? She was lucky he hadn't choked the life out of the overfed mutt. And without the litter of pedigree pups, the Mates for Mates crap didn't have a hope.

His hand pumped faster, recalling the moans of the poisoned dogs. Kill the whole fucking lot of them. His breath caught. *Fuck*. They wouldn't have suffered, simply drifted off to an eternal snooze. *Christ*. His balls were on fire. Ironic.

None of this would have happened if she'd kept her nose away from his shit. Yep, this fire, all Sam's fault. He couldn't believe his luck when Jenna's brat snuck into the barn. *Ooh, furry cuddles*. Left to him, the kid would have toughened up fast.

Killing came easily, though he'd never murdered a kid, but now he'd come close. He rolled his lips and pumped faster. A world of possibilities to explore. Raising his hand, Baxter licked away the pre-cum and chuckled. *Big fucking girl makes me sick*.

Scared he might have said the last words aloud, he checked for any noise. A sign they'd discovered him. His attention snapped to the barn door. *Damn*. Everything had been going well until Soldier Boy stumbled out of the barn, bundle in his arms, and buckled at the knees.

Struggling to see clearly through the fresh snow clinging to his eyelashes, Baxter stepped further away from the safety of the tree line. The boy. His cock softened in his pants as his blood pressure soared.

What a drama. Flames licked the walls and hissed across the roof. He tucked everything neatly back inside his pants and pulled up the zipper. Pity he'd have to finish himself off later. Give Jenna one final poke. If he could stomach it.

Sirens blaring, engines revved, fire trucks and ambulances forced a path through the snow. If he stayed front row much longer, they would spot him.

Driving to Jenna's, he switched on the CB radio. News of the fire already jammed the frequencies, arson on everyone's lips. *You betcha, muppets*.

He kicked open Jenna's door. Bitch hadn't made it home yet, so he grabbed a beer and stretched out on the sofa, inhaled deeply, and pictured the barn in all its smoky glory. A part of him felt cheated. Sure, setting fire to stuff had a magnificent finality, but it didn't turn him on as much as close work. The thrill when you smelled your victim's death. Witnessed life leave their eyes.

Baxter glanced at the clock over the fireplace. Jenna should be home soon, in time to make him supper before he... Hadn't quite figured out her perfect end. He hated Ms Goody Gums. He'd taken pity on her, fucked her hard, but she constantly mooned over her dead husband. Pathetic. Jenna didn't deserve him. Later, before he left town, he'd do her one last favour and dig her broken heart out of her chest.

CHAPTER TWENTY-FIVE

Sam flinched as Snake tried to ease her jumper over her head. "Sorry, you do it. Then let's get you comfortable." Arms drawn close to his side, Snake waited for her to make the next move.

Doc said the meds he'd prescribed might make her drowsy, and she'd nodded off a few times during the drive home from the hospital, dark on him ever since she complained of chest pains and trouble breathing, and he'd refused let her shrug off getting checked in Emergency.

Sam raised her arms. "Thanks, my ribs are sore."

"You coughed a lot." When did she ever complain? Didn't mean he wasn't concerned. He had to touch her, make sure she was okay. Carefully, he pulled the jumper over the head of the most independent woman he'd ever met. The flip side of Sam's gutsy personality, the vulnerable part he'd glimpsed when they kissed. That part scared him shitless.

During the last few months, he was pretty sure he had fallen in love with her, couldn't wait to share how much he cared for her with those closest to him. Sounded simple. Too fast? Some might swear he'd lost his sodding mind, but not the people who meant the most. Not his Sentinel brothers.

Doc had fallen for Kate as soon as he laid eyes on her; Knight, the same, when he'd met Lily. Spanner and Crystal circled around each other, but everyone accepted they were next down the aisle. Hell, it wouldn't surprise him if he showed for training one morning and they'd eloped.

Men of action, their profession, left no room for fart-arsing around. Same went for their personal lives. Commitments made. Decisions held. Convincing the prickly woman who had his heart in her hand that they could have a future together wouldn't be easy, so he'd start by asking her out. A proper date—get to know her better. Nice and slow until she agreed to give him a chance.

Stop right there. End the fairy tale. Nix the happy ending. Sam had a life. He hadn't told her about Knight's offer, but why would she give up everything she'd fought to achieve in the UK to slip away with him to New York? Yeah, in his head, he'd accepted Knight's offer. They each had their own path. No room to manoeuvre. Knight had put his trust in the right man.

"There, better?" His hands skimmed the front of her bra. The small, perfect nipples he couldn't stop thinking about pebbled under his fingers. "Oops, sorry."

"Uh, huh?"

"Yeah, well. Guess you'd be more comfortable without the jeans, too?"

No shake of the head. No words, just her hand placing his palm flat against her belly. So, he undid the zipper, pulled the jeans over her legs, and tossed them to join the jumper in a pile by the bed.

His fucking heart flipped and rolled.

For the sake of both their blood pressures, he stopped short of ripping off her underwear and reached for the pyjamas hanging over the chair. Pink, fluffy jobs with… "Poodles. I'd have thought bulldogs were more your style."

"Grr." She bared her perfectly white teeth.

"Fuck. It's good to see you, er, smile? Come on, into bed." He pulled back the duvet, reached for a pillow to tuck behind her head.

"Snake?"

"Yeah. I'm not going anywhere."

"Oh, okay, great, but I was going to say, the inside of my mouth tastes awful. Do you mind getting me a drink?" A frown crossed Sam's forehead as if he'd suddenly started speaking in tongues.

Twat. "What? No. Course not. You need to take your pills. I'll get a glass of water, or do you prefer juice? There's apple, maybe orange, in the fridge." The cutest grimace wrinkled her face. "Okay. Apple it is."

"I'd prefer whisky."

"Fraid not with those beasties. Tea?"

"Suppose so. Thanks."

He pulled the quilt up to her chin. "Stay warm."

The kettle boiled. Snake grabbed a cup from the shelf and scratched his head. He'd never have guessed there were that many teas on the planet. A jumble of boxes and jars stared at him. Not big on the herbals himself, but he recognised a few names. Chamomile should work. He dunked the bag a few times until the water turned a murky yellow.

Steam billowed from the cup as he stood mesmerised in the bedroom doorway. Sleeping Beauty had nodded off. Free from the tight ponytail she favoured when working, her thick, wavy hair cascaded over the pillow. He imagined strands of the mane gliding over his chest as she rode him fast and hard. Snake cleared his throat, placed the cup on the bedside table, and curled his fingers lightly around Sam's wrist. Pulse strong. Breathing fine.

Bloody hell! Enough, already. Snake drove her mental. Almost lost his bundle when she'd insisted on leaving the hospital. She wasn't made of glass.

Jim wanted to help, too, but at Snake's first snap and growl, he tossed him the one-finger salute and disappeared. Presumably heading straight for the sanctity of his caravan. *Lucky Jim.*

Jenna had ignored Tom's pleas to let him stay with the pups, insisting he go home to shower and sleep. From the lines creasing her forehead and the way Jenna's whole body trembled, smothering hugs were coming Tom's way, too.

The kid surrendered, but not before hero Snake promised to collect him early the next morning. Game, set, and match to team Jenna after he threw a return FIFA match onto the table. The cranky teenager worshipped Snake. Deep in Sam's gut, something stirred, so piece by piece, she re-erected her boundaries. Kids plus lovers equalled danger.

"Hey, still want your tea?" Snake squeezed her hand.

She'd closed her eyes for a minute and sensed him creeping up on her again. And what was it with the sudden touchy-feely stuff? Anyone would think she'd died, not fainted. And no way would she lust after his sweet bod again. Even if his kiss sizzled on her lips. Left her craving more. For the first time since the Ed hell, she caught herself wondering how to allow a man closer than ten paces. And that could not happen.

She snatched her hand away and felt her damn silly insides wobble. Must be the loss of his body heat that turned her bedroom into a fridge. "I'm tired, Snake, and I'm guessing you need sleep as much as I do." She tipped her chin at the door, only half hoping he'd take the hint and head for bed.

"I'm going," he said. "But first you will take these." Tiny blue capsules sat in his palm. Were they big enough to settle jerky nerves? "I'll crash on the sofa. If you need anything. Anything. Sing out."

There's an offer. "Okay, okay. Give them to me. I'll take them in a minute. Without the tea."

"I'd believe you, if your eyes didn't say different." He grabbed her hand and blew on the inside of her wrist. "Glad you're feeling better. Now swallow them and sleep."

With an exaggerated huff, she swallowed the pills and slid under the duvet. "Satisfied?"

"Until the next time."

Honestly? She didn't have the energy for their usual banter. "Go. Out of my bedroom." She needed some time in the dark to think, figure out what to do next. How she'd rebuild. "Night. Thanks for your help." She turned over and tossed the words over her shoulder.

"Goodnight, Sam. Remember, I'm not far away."

Sam leaned into the gentle stroke of his hand on her cheek. *Too late. That door has closed.*

CHAPTER TWENTY-SIX

Snake left the bedroom door open in case Sam woke and needed something, anything. Him—all night. If that was what it took. Five more minutes inside that barn and none of them would have survived. Best he hit the sofa before he changed his mind, turned around, and climbed into bed beside her. Held her tight. A wave of nausea rolled over him, like it did every time he imagined losing Sam.

Knight required an update before they made their next move. Still hyped, unable to sleep, he detoured to the kitchen, opened the fridge. Thankful for the beer that jumped into his outstretched hand, he pulled out his phone and called the boss.

"How's Sam? You back at her place?" Knight asked.

Snake could hear Lily in the background. Although he couldn't make out the words, he guessed she was hanging to hear the news.

"Tell Lily Sam's okay, sleeping now. I'm sure she'll call her tomorrow."

"Hear that, darling? Your mate's doing fine."

"Thanks, Snake. Don't you take your eyes off her. I'm holding you personally responsible for Sam's safety." Lily's voice echoed down his phone. "And don't take any of her nonsense, either. Like her furry friends, her bark is worse than her proverbial bite. 'Night."

"'Night, Lily. I'm here for as long as Sam needs me." Snake wondered what he'd just promised and waited for Knight to quit the rustling and come back to their call.

"Okay. She's gone. What do you want to do?" Knight asked.

"The house is still standing, but there's shit all security. I'll fix that before I leave. The working area is a fucking disaster. Whoever set fire to the barn was serious about causing maximum harm. The kind where people lose their lives. Ask me, it's a no-brainer who started it, but proving it might be more difficult."

"This Baxter knob?"

"Yeah. The man's a psychopath. I want to bring Sam to London. Have her stay with me or put her up in the flat at HQ."

"Sounds like a plan. Not sure of your chances of convincing her to leave, but have at it. Text me your ETA and I'll make sure the flat is ready if that's what Sam prefers. If there's nothing else, gotta go, Lily's off to book club and I'm on kid duty." Knight cleared his throat.

Snake chuckled. The boss always led into danger. "Roger that, Pop. Later."

He needed a few hours' sleep, energy for the toughest decision he'd ever had to negotiate. Sam leaving the farm. Paramount for her safety.

Small, slim, she had lost weight since the opening, and it worried him she wouldn't stop over five minutes for any meal. Tomorrow, he'd make her a full breakfast. Eggs, bacon, toast, the lot. One hand circling his growling stomach, he stretched out on the sofa and tried to get comfortable. At six-foot-four, he'd slept in worse places.

Outside, the last of the fire engines rolled down the driveway. Out loud, he vowed, "Be ready, Baxter Boy, I'm coming for you."

No stranger to nightmares, Sam finally gave up on sleep. The last time she woke, she vaguely remembered whispering, asking to be held, Snake carrying her to bed. Bundled in his arms like a scared three-year-old wasn't exactly the physical connection she imagined between them.

A snore rumbled in her ear. The arms of a giant teddy bear wrapped tightly around her. Before what happened with Ed, she might have taken advantage of his arousal pressed against the curve of her spine, the closeness she missed.

Perhaps the swiftest exit from living hell involved sex. Great sex. Should she risk it? But Snake's concerned, soothing touch knocked on the door of places that carried a huge keep out sign. Hidden places she shouldn't open. Not if she wanted to hold onto what remained of her sanity.

"You're awake?" Snake's sleepy growl, the shift in his breathing, played havoc with her shaky resolve.

Her cheeks flushed. "Yeah, Einstein, I'm awake. You snore."

"Many women will tell you I don't snore." An unshaven chin scraped across the soft flesh on the top of her shoulder.

"Yeah, well."

"And what's that supposed to mean?"

"Nothing. Except you should see someone about your predilection for the hearing impaired."

"My what?"

"You heard."

"I did, but I can't believe you went there."

Honestly, neither could she. "Where? Predilections or the deaf." Ugh. Sometimes she could be well too clever for her own good. Words rolled off her tongue in a sequence she didn't intend, often regretted. "Yeah. Sorry. Insensitive."

"And some." He chuckled.

Snake hauled his body upright, his gaze skipping the usual peckish scan, and hopped straight to devouring her entire body. But no one should start what they had no clue how to finish. Sam sighed and slapped his solid, heavy, bare thigh, pinning her to the bed. *Heaven save me.* Out of bed and on her feet, a slight wobble sent her arse plonking back on the bed.

"Steady."

Strong fingers kneaded the necklace of tight muscle at the base of her skull.

"Mmm, delicious, and as tempting as this is..." She stroked his erection, tenting the sheet. "I need to shower and do some work."

"You need to take it easy. Doc's orders." Snake's arm swept around her waist. "You sucked in a lot of smoke last night. Lie back. Rest. I have a proposition for you." Light, barely felt kisses peppered the side of her neck.

"Mmm. Great idea." Rest or a proposition. Way too hard for this early in the morning. "Except the police will be here soon, and I want to shower before they arrive. And you promised to fetch Tom."

"That I did. First, breakfast." He sighed. "Need help with that shower?"

"No thanks. I'll be okay if I take my time."

"Yeah. Sure, you will."

Sam had no time to blink before he vaulted over her and stood by the bed. Stretching out his hand, he offered to help her stand. Hesitating proved a huge mistake. Snake shifted his hand behind her back and scooped the other under her legs before she got it together to tell him to rack off. In one skilful sweep, she sank into his arms and they headed for the bathroom.

She grinned and nipped his earlobe. "What's this? You Tarzan, me Jane?"

"Whatever turns you on. I'm up for a little rope work."

"You wish." It had been a long time since she'd played. Teased.

Snake's deep laugh hit her with the force of a meteor. Her breath hitched. Did the man have any clue what dirty pictures spun in her mind? Deciding he must, she buried her grin against the scar on his chest, ignored her nonexistent boobs smashed against him, and relished the idea of screaming *pleasure me.*

Sam nodded at the shower and slid to her feet. Damn if she didn't feel her face flush when her pelvis brushed against his erection. "Thanks for the lift."

His sharp intake of breath, a sign. She'd won this round. Out-of-bounds territory, lowering her guard. Trusting him. She gave him a shove. Stolen kisses meant nothing.

His gaze rested on her pathetic lack of cleavage, turning her knees to jelly, and her heart thanked any god listening that Snake had refused to take a hint.

"Shout out when you're done or want me to scrub your back." His voice rumbled in her ear.

"Dream on, soldier."

"It's airman if we're being picky. And I haven't stopped dreaming since you kissed me."

That earned him a snort. "As I remember, you kissed me."

"Now who's been picky?" He swept his hand in a wide arc, offering her space. "Close the door, Jane, before I beg you to let me join you. I'm happy to wash your hair?"

"Never let go of the dream, Tarzan."

The door closed with a soft click. Sam braced one hand against the towel rail and sank onto the edge of the bath. Hair sticking out in all the wrong places, grey smudges shadowing her eyes. Flushed cheeks. The person staring at her from the mirror opposite resembled a war zone. If she didn't pull herself together, Snake might be her death.

Tell yourself that long and often, and your heart might lose the ear plugs.

As water trickled over her body, Sam admitted there were benefits to showering alone. Like the way her hand could stroke her belly and slip between her thighs. Head resting against the shower wall, soft liquid running over her lips, between her breasts, across her pelvis, her fingers found her clit. *Yes*, she breathed, pinching the tight nub and shuddering a gentle release. No complications.

CHAPTER TWENTY-SEVEN

"I'm not leaving." Sam finally gave up wearing out the living room carpet and settled for brooding on the sofa. Her tiny feet curled underneath her while she gnawed at the knuckles of the hand peeking from the sleeve of her oversized sweater.

Snake tilted his head and stared. The picture should be cute, from any angle, except the frown screwing with her adorable face screamed, *need to make a meal of something*.

He'd gladly present himself on a plate if keeping Sam safe wasn't so fucking serious.

She'd reached for the TV remote a few times only to toss it noisily onto the coffee table, preferring to huff and puff her way through threats that didn't faze him. Right?

"Sam..." He cleared his throat, sank into the space beside her, ignored the shrug, and wrapped his arm around her shoulder. Waited for her next round of protest. Until now, her curses had been all kinds of colourful. The more inventive ones boggled his mind.

Her head relaxed against his chest. A long sigh. Spirits soaring, he walked towards the possibility that she'd accepted his suggestion. Okay, it had been a tad more than a suggestion. Shoot him if wanting her served as barbecued meat sounded unreasonable. Leaving the kennels made sense, and he didn't give a fuck if she didn't want to stay at his place. Sentinel's flat would do the job until they tracked and dealt with the person responsible for the recent mayhem. Why couldn't Sam see this?

She shifted closer and walked her fingers along the length of his thigh. Honey-brown eyes smouldered under sweeping eyelashes. Yes! In with a chance. The blink gave her away.

"This is my home. You can't make me leave!" Sam's shriek hurt his ears. "Sorry, didn't mean to shout, but this place means everything to me." Her whine sounded no better. Sam winced.

And so she fucking should, carrying on like a cranky kid. They both knew she was better than that. "Why are you hell bent on sticking your neck out? Instead of sulking, take the help and keep your head down until we catch the fucking maniac with the box of matches."

Tears glistened in her eyes. The effort of holding onto them turning her blue. His jaw dropped.

"Breathe. Goddammit." He wanted to take her in his arms, kiss her senseless, but if he gave in now, they'd end up in her bed, fucking like bunnies, instead of in her car heading for London. "Pack your bag and quit the waterworks." As a precaution, Snake blocked the open doorway. He didn't plan on leaving without her and didn't care if she wanted to take the whole menagerie with her to London. When he didn't hear her move, he turned, ready for another blast.

Her plush lips fixed in a tight line, Sam strode like a demon princess coming for him. Dark shadows beneath eyes brimming with tears. He flinched, ready to duck, until her hands flew beyond his shoulders and slammed the door closed.

Shit, shit, shit. It blew his mind how someone as small as Sam, hips pressed against his, breasts plastered to his chest, brought his cock from half-mast to full in less time than it took to say her name.

He opened his mouth to tell her how much he admired her stubborn determination to stay and fight her enemy. Beg her to forget the last five minutes and let him take care of her, but her tightly curled fist struck his chest, and his voice went AWOL, followed swiftly by his next breath.

Her shirt flew over her head, annihilating any desire to break free. No bra. *Killer.* A quick flick of the button and zipper and her tight denim jeans dropped over her slender legs and piled at her feet. Smiling as he gasped, struggled to find oxygen, Sam flicked her dainty foot and sent her jeans sprawling under a chair.

Shot and tortured, he had faced evil a thousand times, but confronted by this amazing woman, he'd never been more terrified of dying.

Naked, finally. More than worth the wait. Toned calves and smooth thighs, the swell of her hips. Small, milk-white breasts, tight nipples begging to be worshipped. "I want to touch you," he croaked, vowing to sound stronger next time.

"If you don't, I swear I will scream."

Permission granted, his palm trembled on her belly. *Take it slow,* he told the pinkie finger tracing the crest of her hips.

"Yes. Feels great," Sam gasped.

Mindful of where she anchored her knee, he spread his legs wider before curling his fingers and cupping her soft mount. He slid aside the scrap of lace and smoothed a thumb over her clit and smiled when she shuddered.

Eyes closed, he concentrated on keeping his touch light. The throw and catch of her breath told him everything he needed about how to please her.

His cock twitched. A sudden desire to possess her took hold urging him to tug on the strand of hair teasing the corner of her mouth until she surrendered to his lips.

In one movement, Sam hooked her arms around his neck, wound her legs tightly around his waist, pinning him in her embrace. The electricity pulsing between them registered as knock-the-back-of-his-head-off intense.

Right where he belonged, locked between Sam's thighs, he sucked her bottom lip, hungry for whatever she had in mind. "Talk to me, sweetheart. I need to hear the words. How may I fucking serve?"

Her giggle pleased him as much as her tongue plundering his mouth, probing, until their mingling breaths ratcheted to sharp gasps, racing to a finish he had no intention of her reaching so soon.

She'd learn he was much more than a willing cock, but then her wicked fingers found the bulge in his pants and stroked the length of him. Blood drained from his brain at a speed that left him dizzy. Their shared grin turned to a chuckle as Sam showed him she understood his craving for long and slow.

Surrender had never crossed his mind until Sam took point on the kiss. When they finally broke away, she tucked her head under his chin and sighed. A long, breathy exhale that said much more than words ever shared. Hand on heart, she offered everything he wished for. Touching his lips to her ear, he inhaled her sweet scent. In another life, he'd lay his soul at her feet.

"Better?" he asked.

The sharp nip of her nails digging deep into his shoulders sent shock waves coursing through his body. Cool, slender fingers ran from the base to the tip of his cock. Sam loved to tease, and God help him if he didn't appreciate her efforts. "That's it, sweetheart. Harder. Squeeze." He added a please because begging never hurt. With one hand cupped behind her head, he lowered her mouth to his nipple. "Suck," he commanded. Softly.

Teeth sank into the sensitive flesh.

"Argh. Damn, that feels good." Returning the favour, he nudged her chin with his nose, eased her head upwards, and closed his mouth over her left nipple and moulded the rosy tip with his tongue. Fucking amazing didn't come close to describing the pleasure humming under his skin.

"I hate to play favourites. But don't forget the other one," Sam moaned.

Making sure he took his time getting there, he licked the shallow crease of her cleavage, nuzzled the gentle under-curve of her right breast before latching onto the starved nipple.

"More," she hummed.

Her pelvis ground against the rough denim of his jeans. Her soft groans grew louder. At this pace, she'd be sore later, and he'd cut off his right arm before he hurt her. The move away earned his chin a sharp bite.

"Easy. Let's take this to the bedroom and I'll lose the clothes."

"Getting hot?" She winked and grabbed the front of his shirt.

"Any hotter and you'll see steam come out my ears. Hold tight." He cupped her arse and lifted her higher. A yelp and two seconds later his knees bumped the edge of her bed and she landed in the centre of the duvet. Outstretched hands reached for his belt.

"Allow me." Another five seconds and he'd shed the shirt, ditched the boots, and tossed his jeans and boxers into the corner. Had to be a record. "Shit. Condom?"

"In the drawer. Fucking hell, Snake, move it. I'm losing my soddin' mind."

Me first. His fingers fumbled with the wrapper.

"Give it to me."

Bossy much? Sam loomed above him, snatching the foil package from him and ripping it open. Control fast disappeared from his vocabulary as talented fingers sheathed his cock.

On a deep exhale, he thrust to the hilt and almost came simply from watching her eyelids flutter with pleasure. But Sam's sharp intake of breath scared him. Torn between pulling out of her tight body and a raging desire to keep pounding into her, he stroked her cheek. "Hey, you okay?"

"Oh yes, but give me a sec. You're a lot to take at once," she gasped.

Male ego couldn't let that pass. His pride swelled, eager to show her how amazing he could make this for her.

"All the time you need, sweetheart." His arms and thighs shook with the effort to maintain control.

A breath later, his tantalising beauty slid up and down his length, claiming what she wanted. "Stay still while I fuck you," she murmured.

Happy to let her steal the show for a while, he smiled and placed his hands behind his head. "Not a muscle." For fun, he twitched his pec. Loved it when she gave him that giggle. Moments when Sam let go were precious.

Her hips rose and fell on his engorged cock and that smile kept on giving as she kissed his eyelids, his nose, his mouth. He did his best not to move, but playing the submissive never appealed. Not even for someone as captivating as the woman riding him into fucking oblivion.

The tips of his fingers skimmed her arms, traced the hollows between her ribs, brushed the sides of her breasts. He grabbed Sam's hips and took charge of her undulating pelvis. "You are amazing."

Snake sucked her right nipple between his teeth and nipped. Not too hard, enough to feel the burn.

"John. For the love of…" she pleaded.

Hearing her say his name. Her inner muscles sucked him deeper. He tightened his grip, stopped her from moving on his cock. If he didn't, he'd come first. *And that, my man, is not happening.* Switching nipples, he showered the nub with twice as much attention. Her quiet keening filling the room. Music to his fucking ears.

"John, please."

"Steady, enjoy. I'll give you what you need." He went back to attending to her gorgeous nipple, loving her salty taste.

Sam wriggled, trying to regain control. Her face contorted in a grimace of pain and pleasure he'd never tire of putting there.

He let go of her hips and cupped her face. "Look at me."

Her eyes opened wide, and his soul rose from its dark hole and flew to her side. Faster, harder. He kept up a steady rhythm until her muscles clenched. So fucking tight he could hardly move. Her fingernails raked across his chest, marking him, claiming him.

"John. Fuck. Harder."

Whatever she needed.

"Oh, Go…"

"Come for me, Sam," he begged, certain he couldn't last much longer.

Eyes shining with power and panic that reflected his own, a long, high-pitched scream soared from her lips. This had the power to destroy them, but who the fuck cared?

Her fingers latched onto his hair, tugging on his scalp as his cock kept pumping. There would be no next time, so he held his breath and listened to the woman demanding he keep fucking her.

The power of Sam's orgasm ricocheted through him, tearing his release from the base of his spine. He rode every ripple until it ripped his skull apart and Sam collapsed on his chest. He held her close, her smile tickling the hairs on his chest.

"Fuck me," she groaned.

"Oh, I plan to," he breathed into Sam's smile. "Give me a minute."

No woman came come close to Sam. Inside her, he'd found home. Mistake, the voice in his head warned. *Run.*

Soft grey light shone on the window. Morning. With a long sigh and as much regret, Snake untangled himself from the arms of the sleeping beauty next to him, slipped silently out of bed and into the jeans he had kicked off last night. His socks had gone the way of all lost socks the minute he'd chucked them across the room. Boots in hand, he left the bedroom and went downstairs, careful to dodge the step with the squeak.

Unless on a covert op, he didn't sneak around, but since he'd met Sam, his life overflowed with firsts, and as luck would have it, someone cleared their throat, ruining any idea that he'd gotten away without seeing anyone.

Coffeepot in his hand, Jim stood in the kitchen, the early morning sun bouncing off his shiny bald head. He raised the pot in his direction. "Coffee?"

Sprung. Ashamed. Pissed, that Jim had caught him sneaking away. Snake opened his mouth to suggest where Jim could stick his brew. Instead, he tossed the other man a sheepish tip of the chin and shook his head. "No, thanks."

Jim shrugged and placed the pot on the bench. "Leaving?"

God save him from those with a sixth sense. Jim reminded him of Doc. The team medic, another man who said little, but who had a knack for pressing all the right buttons when he did. "Yep. Early start. Have to return ASAP to London. Duty calls." Jim nodded and made an odd sound, as though he'd sucked in a lie and wanted to spit. Coward he'd swallow but couldn't let liar pass. "Boss called. We're wheels up and heading overseas in twelve hours."

"I see. Sure you haven't got time for that coffee?" Jim offered again.

"Thanks. Tempting, but I'd best be on the road."

"And Sam?" Jim grabbed another mug, his question weighing heavily on Snake's shoulders. "She awake? I'm sure she'd appreciate one before you leave."

Out in the caravan it would be a miracle if Jim had slept through Sam screaming his name, so he didn't bother pretending. "She's still asleep." More throat clearing from them both.

"I thought you planned on taking her to London. Some safe house, right?"

"Nope. She prefers to stay here, with the dogs." All grown up with ability and skills to look after herself. He wasn't happy, but short of chaining her to the back seat of the Jeep, his hands were tied. If she learned to duck quicker, he'd rest easier.

Leaving now seemed like the fair and honourable move. He'd warned Sam sex was complicated. The police were investigating the fire, and Knight had already lined up Trigger to watch out for her until they had the person responsible for the fire behind bars. Keeping Sam safe had to become a Sentinel priority. He trusted

Trigger to do the job, but it wouldn't hurt to ask. "Do me a favour, Jim, and watch out for her? I'm not sure when I'll be back."

"Uh huh. No need to ask. Consider it done. Guess I'll see you sometime."

Jim poured himself another cup of coffee. Dismissed. Snake swallowed the sour taste in his mouth that threatened to hang out for at least the rest of the day.

"Yep. Take care, Jim. Pleasure to have met you."

At the rear door, George lay next to Bounce, his jaw resting on his front paws. With a deep huff, one eye open, he hauled himself up for a morning scratch behind his ears. "Okay, feller, you and your girlfriend enjoy your night out here under the stars?" Snake winked at the German shepherd and hoped George enjoyed his retirement. "Gotta get crackin', boy."

George whined. Snake gave him one last pat and brushed the tear from his eye.

CHAPTER TWENTY-EIGHT

Snake rolled his head and tried without much luck to ease the tension in his neck. They were sitting ducks fixated on locating Seckou. Pity Sam had other ideas, sneaking into every moment, night and day, occupying every breath, awake or asleep. Life had changed since he met her.

Knight stood beside their vehicle. A beat-up lorry to a passing observer who didn't know about the engine with extras. Oumar, their Burkinabe contact, had a knack for hooking them up with the right ride. Snake took off his cap and scrubbed his hand through his sweaty hair. They were all on edge, cursing the wind stirring the dirt, the flies circling over their heads. The boss' pacing didn't help.

"Snake, for Christ's sake, tell me something I want to hear," he said.

"On it, boss. Almost there." Snake shielded his tablet from another dust shower and kept punching the keys. Within seven minutes, less, Seckou's location popped onto his screen. "Got 'im. They're on the move."

"Yeah, yeah. Tell me something I don't know."

"Travelling fast. North, northeast." The intel earned a curse. Not much, but before Snake could pinpoint their prey more accurately, Knight slammed his fist on the map.

"Stone me fucking dead, Snake. That's the airstrip. He's heading for a plane."

"No way," Spanner barked.

"If he takes off, we've lost him. Not something I'm prepared to let happen. Not now. Not this fucking time. This ends today." Checking his weapon as he strode forward, Knight headed to the front of the vehicle. "Spanner, get in. Drive like Satan with the wind at his back and get us to that airstrip before that arsehole is wheels up."

Pumped, the spark lit, Snake drew in a deep breath through his nose. Working with his brothers, depending on each other to bring down the bad guys. This stuff used to be the reason he bothered to get up in the morning. Except one bad-tempered woman had quenched the usual fire in his belly. Refused to rest in the comfort of his soul. If he lived through the next hour, he'd be on the first plane back to her. No more running. He'd lay it all on the line and hope like hell she'd give him a chance.

The lorry rumbled to a stop two clicks from the landing strip. They couldn't risk driving any closer and having Seckou's guards clock them, so they'd move fast despite the lack of cover. In record time, they were out of the vehicle and hanging for Knight's signal.

"Wait up," the boss snarled.

Wait? Wasn't that what they'd been doing the last six months? After years of Seckou evading them anytime they got close, they were in spitting distance and Knight ordered them to twiddle their thumbs and shuffle their feet. *Say again?*

"What's up, boss?" Doc asked, beating Snake to it.

"You suddenly lost the ability to speak English? Wait. Means don't do another fucking thing until I give the order."

Knight's jaw locked. A profile of solid determination. No room for error etched in his furrowed brow. The most important mission of their lives, their ticket to finally burying Mike in their hearts and the ground. One final push. Annihilation imminent. No one moved.

"Two vehicles approaching. Copy?" Knight alerted them.

Danger present. More numb nuts.

"Copy that." Spanner replied, then tapped his mic to mute. "Snake, you and Sam? Are you two serious?"

"Are you shitting me?" Where the hell did Spanner think they were?

Spanner shrugged. "Crys bet me you are. I said no way, but then I thought maybe…"

"Shut up. Terrorist on the loose." Snake lowered his voice and tamed the fist, wanting to break Spanner's jaw.

"Just don't muck it up, okay? Crys will kill you." Spanner reactivated comms.

Seriously?

Knight secured the last tab on his Kevlar vest. Staying low, weapon at his shoulder, he moved in, trying to getter a bead on what the hell was going on inside the hangar.

"Okay. Let's go get this fucker." He signalled for them to follow.

Knight and Doc led, leaving him and Spanner to provide cover, check for any sneaky sniper shit. The boss reached the opening to the hanger first and pulled the pin on a tear gas cannister. Smoke without mirrors. An acrid cloud, thick enough to blind, while they slipped in before the enemy could retaliate.

The tossers covered their faces. Splutters and coughs rattled around the space. Trained to operate in this kind of attack, Snake grinned and swallowed the bitter taste flooding his mouth.

"Two tangos, two o'clock," Knight warned.

"Got 'em," Spanner replied and took the shots. A series of quick pops "Two down."

"Target on the move," Doc confirmed.

Weapon raised, Seckou, the idiot, ran, firing directly at them. Knight swerved right, Doc to the left. Their footsteps echoed across the airstrip.

Snake swivelled on his heel and copped the nearest knob'ed an elbow to the throat. The gratifying crack and gurgle as the enemy struggled to breathe went a long way to improving his shitty mood. Another lurched from the darkness and ran straight into his other fist. The blow sent the fucker reeling, blood seeping from his broken nose.

He checked Spanner. Doing okay, no help needed. He almost missed the glint in his side vision. *Bollocks.* A knife. *Shouldn't have brought that baby to play today.* His laugh bordered on overkill, but letting shit out showed Dickhead how much he'd ruined Snake's day. A sharp flick of the arsehole's wrist and his weapon tumbled from his hand. The follow-up to the gonads sent a satisfying scream winging its way to his ears. He took pleasure in the extra wrench to the hand and whispered in the dickhead's ear. "Had enough?"

"*Va au diable.*"

"Go to hell. Guaranteed, mother fucker, *mais pas aujourd'hui.*" Or any day soon if he could help it. A kick to the guts and all insurgents were done. He secured their hands with zip ties and spotted Seckou across from him running towards a smaller hangar. Snake took off after him. Every fibre, every blood cell in his body was focused on bringing him down. For Mike. For his team.

He didn't have to check that Spanner had his six. If not him, one of the others. Feet flying, he kept running. Inside the hangar, he ducked behind a tower of boxes and listened for any clue to where Seckou hid. A noise above alerted him to the small staircase. Weapon aimed above his head, he took the stairs two at a time and caught Seckou standing in the middle of a no-exit mezzanine. *Gotcha.*

Below, a scrimmage erupted. Spanner could take care of them, but a series of gunshots and Knight's yell made him hesitate.

"Two cars," Knight boomed in his earpiece.

With a yell, Seckou made his move and dived for him, two hands fixed on a handgun he tried desperately to embed in Snake's face.

"That all you got, you piece of shit?" It didn't take long to wrestle and pin Seckou to the ground. Any terrorist leader he'd ever met put on weight while they sent their minions off to do the dirty work. He rammed the butt of his own gun into Seckou's face. *Hurts, doesn't it?*

Seckou's spit hit him dead centre between the eyes. "Bollocks." The terrorist bit his forearm and Snake saw red. Jacked up and fucking dangerous, he punched Seckou again and again, but the fucker kept on coming, his hand clawing beneath him, searching for a weapon long gone. Defeated, Seckou went limp, heavy in the grip Snake had on the front of his tunic.

Heavy boots clanged on the stairs as the rest of the team charged to help.

"You okay?" Knight asked, nodding at the gurgling man hanging off the end of his arm.

"Fantastic, boss. Seckou neutralised. Where were you?"

"Hilarious. Good job. Now shut the fuck up and let's get this piece of shit out of here."

Snake chuckled at all the praise he'd ever need and holstered his weapon. Too soon. Seckou reached inside his tunic for...

Snake didn't wait to find out. He snatched his weapon from his holster and popped three shots into the terrorist, two to the chest, one to the brain, before he had time to blink.

CHAPTER TWENTY-NINE

Friday, D Day. How the hell Lily found a bloody yoga class in Giggleswick would remain a bloody mystery.

"Hurry, Sam, the class starts in half an hour, and you still haven't changed," Lily hollered up the stairs.

"What? I can't wriggle on a mat dressed this way?" Towel covering her girly bits, she leaned over the top railing. Lily's eyes popped open, wider than should be humanly possible.

"You are joking! Put some clothes on right now."

"Yes, mum." Happy to play naughty, she poked her tongue out and gave Lily a quick flash. Unfortunately, nothing budged Lily once she'd made up her mind. "What does a girl wear for this torture? I don't own any pink ballet tights."

"Funny. Don't tell me you don't own yoga pants and a loose T-shirt because I've seen you lolling around in those more times that I care to remember. Just cross your heart and promise you won't wear your fave tee. The one with chocolate ice-cream stains on the front." She waved her hand. "Come on, Sam. You said you'd come, and I'm not letting you change your mind because Snake is here."

"Witch," Sam murmured. Now that Lily mentioned it, she

couldn't deny that hopping back into bed with Snake had a lot more going for it than soddin' yoga. He'd arrived a few days ago, here to see George, or so he said, and hadn't left. Yet.

The lorry rumbled to a stop two clicks from the landing strip. They couldn't risk driving. "If you prefer, I have gear you can borrow," Lily said.

"Great." The hairs on the back of her neck snapped to attention when Snake snuck behind her. His arousal pressing against her arse. Sam jabbed her elbow into his ribs.

"Don't go. Stay with me. I'm sure I can twist you into a few positions to raise your consciousness." Snake's nose nuzzled behind her ear.

"Mmm. Tempted." If he meant more of what they shared last night, she'd be more than happy to go a second round.

any closer and having Seckou's guards clock them, so they'd move fast despite the lack of cover.

"I heard that," Super-ears cried out. "Snake, leave her alone. She's mine."

"Want me to fight her to the death?" Snake growled in her ear.

"Absolutely." Hell, she practically purred.

Snake chuckled, caught her wrist, and kissed the tips of her fingers. "Or give it a go. You might enjoy it. Help you relax."

"I am relaxed. Believe me." Nothing had happened since the fire, and slowly the kennels were getting back to normal. Tom and Jenna hadn't been around much lately, but she hoped they'd visit over the weekend. She stroked the stubble on Snake's chin. "Give me five, Lily." She turned and wiggled her way to the bedroom. One day soon, she'd show him how much she adored that twinkle in his eye.

"Jeez, woman. Do you know what you do to me?" Snake stalked after her.

"Stay where you are, or I will never leave the house." Ten minutes later, she'd dressed in her cleanest slob-around-the-house gear and joined Lily at the bottom of the stairs.

"At last. Are you ready to meet the guru?" Lily asked, swinging a rubber tube over her shoulder.

"What the heck is that?" Sam stared at the wobbly weapon.

"Yoga mat. Don't worry, you can borrow one at the hall."

"Hall? How many people is this guru of yours expecting?"

"Not sure. Guess we'll find out."

Snake caught her hand before she could follow Lily. His nose grazed the side of her neck. She sighed, knowing how much she'd rather play bendy doll at home.

"See you soon. Trigger will be there, watching out for you both." His light kisses peppered a line from her neck to her jaw.

"Yeah, yeah. I'd argue, but there's no way Knight will let Lily go without protection."

"Him and me, both. Now be a good girl and watch that ankle."

"Good? You wish." Her ankle had been well healed for a while. His last kiss, firm against her lips, made it almost impossible to leave. At the bottom of the stairs, she turned and watched him wave goodbye.

"Yeah, yeah. Remember, you said you'd feed the dogs." She returned his wave, puzzled by how quickly they'd become a couple.

"So, what do you think? Great class, right?" Lily cocked her head to one side.

"Yeah, relaxing." Unexpected, considering the mixed bag of bodies who'd shoved themselves into positions that shouldn't be humanly possible.

She always enjoyed time with Lily and the way they laughed at themselves. Something Sam hadn't done in a long time. Let down her guard. Been honest about how she felt. Speaking of feelings, denying her body's response to Snake, the pleasure, passion he evoked with the tip of his finger was pointless.

Secure in his arms, Sam felt truly at home. But with that came the flashbacks, a return to emotions, locations that still caused trouble. Last night, after they'd made love, she'd been a tick away from surrendering into what her soul had already figured out. She loved him and wished she could trust, share. But she couldn't give her heart only to lose it again.

Snake lived for his job. Every time he went on a mission, she'd worry he might wind up keeping Ed company. No matter how many times he called, texted he'd be home. In her mind lurked the day when Knight came to the house and told her Snake wouldn't be coming back to her.

Sam clutched her chest and gasped. Arash's face blazed in front of her, then flew into the smoke. Déjà vu. A pain, but these days, it rarely took her completely by surprise.

"You okay? Here, have some water?" Lily tilted her water bottle towards her.

"Er. No. Yes. Let's check out the juice bar." She'd seen the counter surrounded by a few chairs in the entrance when they arrived.

"Sounds splendid to me, but sure you're okay? You look kind of peaky."

"Yes, nurse. I'm fine. I need sugar and you're paying."

One sip of the extra large carrot and apple juice and the world sat at a better angle. Sam leaned back and got scared when the creak meant the plastic seat might collapse like the day in the café when Snake had been such a grump.

Lily laughed, then shrieked when her chair folded underneath her. Sam stretched out her hand. "Aha, karma."

It took her friend a second or two to stop laughing and grab her hand.

"Oh, sorry. Are you okay?" the young girl called out from behind the counter.

"She's fine." Sam shoved the piece of carrot cake she'd insisted on ordering in front of Lily. Elbows on the table, her head bobbed at the edge. "Get that down you. Guaranteed to cure every ache and pain. Don't believe me? Ask Doc."

Lily stayed standing and stuck her plastic fork into the cream cheese icing and beamed. "I can't say no. Speaking of delicious things." She winked. "You and Snake seem to get along very well."

Fucking understatement. "Sure. He's fun."

"Fun?"

"Useful." That sounded a lot better. "Good with hands—great at mending fences." *Shit, this is getting worse.*

"Oh, come on. If Kate were here, she'd call you out. I'd say you were falling for the man."

"And you'd be wrong. We're friends, fuck buddies. That's all." Married to alpha hunk Knight, Lily should be over blushing.

"Aside from making love, do you ever talk? Have you told him what happened?"

"No, Lily. It hasn't come up. You going to eat that?" Raising her fork, she made a stab at Lily's cream cheese icing. "He'll be gone soon. We'll probably lose contact. He said last night that Knight man offered him his dream job in New York. Fantastic opportunity. I suggested he book the flight." Sam nosedived into the glass of juice. Lily didn't need to see her choking on unshed tears. "When Knight goes away on a job, do you worry?" she had to ask.

"All the time, but we've talked about it a lot. I understand. After all, Daniel accepts all my spikey insecurities, bites his tongue when I work on the midwife programme in Africa. Our men look out for each other, and I trust he's in excellent hands. As for Snake taking the job in New York, a little bird tells me he may regret being there on his own."

Our men. Never again. "You must stop talking to bloody birds, Lily. People might think you've lost the plot."

"Says the girl who celebrates her dog's birthdays. Wears a funny hat and everything."

"If not me, who?" Sam laughed. She missed their days together at college, snuggled on the sofa, drinking wine, yelling at B-grade movies. "And speaking of predators." Which they weren't, but it seemed to fit. She nodded at the revolving door. "Isn't that Big Bird?"

"What?" Lily's head swivelled round.

Sam couldn't see her face but judging from the quick rise and fall of her shoulders, she hadn't expected to see Knight heading straight for them.

"Daniel? What are you doing here? Is Mary okay?" Knight steadied her as she shot out of her seat.

"Easy, sweetheart. All good. Mary's fine. Snake is outside in the car, giving her a bottle." He couldn't hide his chuckle.

"Okay." Her friend didn't look very sure. "What's up?"

"I'm needed in London, pronto. Sorry, Lily, I wish things were different. I hate to cut our visit short, Sam."

Knight brushed a strand of Lily's hair behind her ear and Sam sighed. Couldn't help it. Time stood still whenever these giant alphas showed tenderness. Precious moments. Sentinel men had scary skills, prepared to put down the bad guy at all costs. Stuff, many believed, that only happened in the movies.

"Sam, Trigger went back to the kennels. Snake insisted on taking you home. He's outside. Okay, ladies. We ready?"

CHAPTER THIRTY

Snake scooped Sam off her feet and stumbled through the doorway of the outbuilding where Sam kept extra supplies. "Wow, you've got a lot heavier during the last few hours." He grinned. "Amazing how hungry a yoga class makes a person." Sam had scoffed her pizza with extra mushrooms and guilt-eyeballed him until he'd shared his last slice.

"Bloody cheek, put me down or I won't show you where I hide the beer." She squeezed his bicep. "The wonders of modern plastic?"

Snake loved Sam's laugh. Despite everything that had happened, she took it all in her stride.

The repairs were going well, and since he and Trigger were staying at the kennels, there'd been no more trouble, but most days, he saw past Sam's brave face, noticed when she hesitated when she left a building, looking around corners before she reached them.

hey hadn't talked about it, but they agreed. Wait. For what, he hadn't figured out.

More than once during the drive home he'd thought of pulling over—his foot even nudged the brake a few miles back—and taking her into his arms. Convincing her nothing would happen, that he'd do anything to keep her safe.

"Put me down, idiot, before we fall, and I break my bloody neck." Sam's icy breath curled in ribbons over his head.

"Never. Not in my arms. Locked to me. Where you belong." He nibbled her earlobe. Her mix of shriek and smile was intoxicating. "You're mine."

"Stop. I'm not sure we need any more beer." Sam waved her finger in his face. "Save your alpha for George."

He licked the tip of her finger and sucked it into his mouth. Sam buried her laugh in his neck. A direct hit to his blood pressure gauge as he stumbled and his shin hit a low-lying object.

Sam's arm flayed to the side, clipping the tip of his nose. "Shh. You'll wake Trigger. Move your head. I'm trying to turn on the light."

"Brilliant idea. I agree, I don't need any beer. Let's skip it and head back to the house. To bed."

"Look out," Sam cried.

Too late, his feet slid from under him. *Way to go, hero.* With a grunt, he threw his weight to the side, flipping Sam on top of him at the last minute. His spine hit the concrete slab with a hard slap, taking the brunt of the fall.

Sam screamed.

"Hey, I'm sorry. Did I hurt you?"

Eyes glazed, no words, but his stomach rolled at the frantic shaking of her head. Jim sat slumped against an old double-door fridge. An open beer bottle in his hand. Blood dripped from his lips. Locked in a mix of sadness and disbelief, his eyes stared at nothing. Life's last hope caught in a contorted smile.

Before he could stop her, Sam scrambled from underneath him and checked for Jim's pulse. Going through the motions, nothing more. The man had died hours ago.

"Jim. Look at me. It's Sam. Please." One hand on top of the other, her tiny palms pressed hard on the wound in Jim's chest. "It's going to be okay. Open your eyes."

Her sobs ripped through him. Gently, he pried her fingers from Jim's shirt and brought them to sit over his heart. "Leave it, sweetheart. He's gone."

"No. Call an ambulance. Come on, Jim. Stay with me."

Sam refused to give up on Jim. She scanned his body, running the checks, searching for any flutter of breath to prove Snake had it wrong and her friend lived. Desperate to keep the hurt buried inside, she swallowed the truth.

Jim shouldn't be dead, but a hunting knife lay by the body. The arrogant bastard who'd murdered him had tossed it there. Why? Everyone loved the man who minded no one's business but his own and who had been her rock this past year. "Christ, look at his head."

Revealing bone, the deep cut had almost severed Jim's head from his body. It shouldn't be this hard to breathe. Not sure what else to do, she gripped Snake's forearm, needing answers, for him to make sense of the madness dragging her further into the black hole she'd been circling for years.

Snake eased the knife from her trembling fingers and brought her blood covered hand to his chest. She shuddered, unable to stop her strangled sobs striking out into the night. "Who did this?" Their eyes met. "Baxter. I'll kill him."

"Sit." Snake ordered. "Sam, listen to me…"

His voice drifted further away. The edges of her vision blurred. Eyes closed, she strained to hear him, find an anchor, before the flashbacks snatching at her heart, dragged away all her reason.

Not fucking now. Jim needed her. Three sharp exhales steadied her nerves before she fumbled in her pocket for her phone. "We need an ambulance, police," she heard herself say. *Yes, in control now.*

Snake caught her wrist and shook his head. "Easy. I've got it. Come with me."

Together they returned to the house. Pressed against the side of

Snake's solid chest, she could breathe, think. Pulling herself together proved a challenge, hell, a struggle, but she had to keep it together. The dogs were barking. As soon as she opened the door, they whined, instantly sensing something had shifted in the world. Bounce licked her hand while George nudged in between them and forced them apart.

On TV, people offered cops a tea and a biscuit. Floyd sighed when none appeared and signalled for his sergeant, Temple, a sickly looking git, to open his notebook. Rank had its privileges—no more word-for-word scribbles for him.

"I wonder who this guy pissed off?" Temple sighed and scratched his head, flicked the edge of a torn curtain looking for fingerprints on the ledge Floyd knew weren't there.

No sign of a struggle, which meant the murderer had surprised good ole Jim. Unusual. According to Miss Leigh, the victim had been in the military. True what they said, retirement slowed you down. He looked forward to it.

Whoever had done this had grabbed the unsuspecting sod and plunged a knife straight into his heart. Quick. Silent. Intentional. Didn't need no coroner to confirm.

The kennels were in the middle of fucking nowhere, no neighbours. Only this poor man's screams disturbing the night. Some guy, called Trigger, had been home, tucked up with the dogs. He'd had no reason to come out there and had heard nothing unusual. Not surprising. Looked like this guy had been dead for a while.

Blood slashed an uneven path across the concrete floor to a noisy fridge, where the murderer had staged the body. A last minute touch, the beer in his hand. A sick toast to hearts beating strong in the afterlife. In his career, Floyd hadn't come across many of this type of madman.

For the benefit of the big guy with his protective arm around the woman's waist, Floyd hooked the tip of his pencil under the sleeve of Jim's jacket. They didn't need to be there, but Miss Leigh had insisted on coming when he went to examine the body. "No defensive wounds, no sign of a struggle."

For longer than Floyd could remember, blood failed to impress. Held no more shock factor than the dogs he bet on who failed to run anywhere but last at the track. Different for Temple, for whom the more graphic, wet bits of their work were a challenge. Fist pressed to his upper lip, the sergeant loped from the room.

They all raised an unimpressed eyebrow, including the woman. Tough, not a wince or a tear. They didn't make women like they used to, and that was a fucking shame.

"Good help is hard to find." Floyd jerked his chin at his plonker sergeant and fished a pair of sterile blue gloves from his pocket. The tangy stench of blood hit his nostrils as he bent over the body and hovered his index finger over what was left of the man's throat. "Bit hard to see."

"A minute." The woman stepped behind him and flicked a switch.

Light flooded the room, followed by Miss Leigh's scream piercing his fucking eardrums.

"What the hell?" The big guy sprang to her side and surrounded her with a protective cuddle.

Nothing like a murder to pull people together. Lloyd smiled at the cosy couple and scratched his head. Yep. Retirement couldn't come too soon. He'd been doing this job far too long.

"Sir?" Temple returned and stood staring at the words smeared red on the cracked mirror behind the half-open door.

Now look at what you made me do. You're next, Sam.

Floyd had to hand it to their murderer. If this didn't make Miss Leigh run, she had iron tits. Judging by the way the big guy's fingers twitched on her arm, like some fucked up morse code, Lloyd had only scratched the surface on what was going on here. "I'd like you both to come to the station and give your statements. Temple will organise for you to look at photofits. See if you recognise someone who may have been hanging around the kennels. Do you have CCTV footage, Miss Leigh? Any outdoor cameras?"

"Er, no."

"You sure? I thought I noticed a camera."

"Yes, there are two, but they're not operational."

The big guy grunted. Didn't take much to get his meaning. Why bother having the things if they didn't work?

"Could our statements wait, officer?" he asked, stepping in front of Miss Leigh, who didn't seem, interestingly, to appreciate the man's concern.

"Sorry, sir. Your name again." Floyd nodded at Temple, double-checking that he recorded it.

"Snake. John Smith." He took a breath, waited for the inevitable disbelief to ripple over his face. Floyd couldn't be bothered to satisfy. "I really don't see…"

And I really couldn't care the fuck less. "Yes, sir. I realise it's late. We'll keep it brief. I'm happy for you and Miss Leigh to take your vehicle and follow us to the station. Now. Sir. The sooner we leave, the quicker you can return home."

John Smith took a step towards him, but before shit could get ugly, Floyd swept out into the night expecting them all to follow.

CHAPTER THIRTY-ONE

"You okay?" Snake kissed the top of Sam's head.

"Yeah, I'm fine." Her tone didn't convince him, but he didn't push it.

She'd been unusually quiet since they left the station. Floyd had taken his time questioning them, going over and over the same shit, treating them as suspects. Finally, Snake had insisted the prick of a detective charge them or allow them to leave.

Adjusting his rear-view mirror gave him an excuse to glance at Sam. Too pale, exhausted. When they got home, he'd take her in his arms, pray she didn't protest, and hold her, but right now the clenched fists banging against her knees said she wouldn't appreciate being smothered.

The tight squeak of the handbrake confirmed they'd made it home, but Sam didn't move, so he opened his door, eased out of his seat, and strolled to the passenger side. "Sam."

She turned. Eyes filled with tears stared at him. Her trembling bottom lip shredded emotions he tried damn hard to keep under wraps, so he cleared his throat and held out his hand. Lights were on in the outbuilding. They'd taken Jim's body to the morgue, but forensics were still collecting evidence. Sam gasped.

"Come here." Snake turned his body to block where Jim had died, pulled her against his chest, and slipped his hand around her waist. They hurried up the stairs onto the veranda. "Go on in. I'll be there in a minute."

"Where's Trigger?"

"Inside. I'll take care of the dogs and call Knight. Give him the latest while you get warm. When I get back, we can eat, drink, talk? Whatever you like."

"I'd like you to stop treating me as though I'll break." She flashed him a half-smile. "After you feed the dogs, I want you to fuck me into the middle of next week. Make me forget, Snake. Please."

Seeing Sam struggling almost finished him. Two steps and he cradled her face in his hands. Suddenly, he understood what thumbs were for, swiping away her tears.

"My dogs won't starve, Snake." Her voice, low and husky, convinced him.

Pleasing Sam was etched in his DNA. He circled her wrists with his fingers and pulled her to him. "Come with me." He opened the door, and they practically fell up the stairs, tossing off coats and boots as they went.

"How'd it go?" Trigger yelled from the living room.

"Later, mate," he answered, lassoing Sam's neck with his scarf.

"Bend over. Put your hands against the wall," Snake commanded.

Sam's breath hitched. The way the raw edges of his deep baritone broke through his smile melted the iron grip on her insides. Too many people she loved were dead. Out of answers and not sure she'd have the strength to get out of bed in the morning, she did as Snake asked, happy for him to have control.

Pressing her palms firmly against the bedroom wall, she shifted her weight to her heels and arched her spine. *Bless Lily and her yoga class.*

Snake pushed her jeans over her hips, past her knees. "Spread your legs. Wider."

Sam lifted her feet and freed the denim from her ankles. Next, he rolled her underwear over her thighs and pressed his arousal against her. Too slow. She opened her mouth to scream at him for messing around, order him to get on with the job. Take off some fucking clothes.

His breath tickled the inside of her ear, then wandered, wet and warm, along the length of her neck. *Yes.* Sam moaned and reached around his hip and helped his fingers undo the button and zipper of his jeans. Desperate to touch him, stroke his erection.

"You're killing me, Sam."

"Not before I lose my mind. Do you always go commando?" Funny thing, life. Right now, the best part? Snake wore no underwear. She couldn't resist a gentle squeeze of the soft, silky balls caressing her palm.

"That's it. Feel me, Sam. I'm so fucking hard for you. I can't keep my hands off you."

Rough fingertips caressed the outside of her thighs. Already, the smell of sex filled the room. *Wonderful.* The line of unshaven stubble on his chin grazed the top of her shoulder and she shivered. Every breath she took shuddered through her. Erratic, frantic. "What are you waiting for? Yes." Sam sighed her approval at the sound of his jeans sweeping the floor to join hers in the corner.

His cock rubbed the slit between her arse cheeks and a finger found her clit. Magic. Her world shrank to a tiny, manageable ball. She tried to turn. To fuck him. *Make love?* Blood pounded in her skull. More than an outstanding fuck, Snake treated her as though she meant everything to him. Made it his sometimes infuriating mission to keep her safe.

When had it started? Wanting, needing Snake in her life.

Two fingers slipped inside her, swiftly followed by a third. "Oh, shi…"

"Breathe. I've got you." Snake's arm tightened around her waist.

"I want you." Three short words hung at the entrance of the cave that housed her heart. "Inside me. Now." Best to clarify.

Breath caught in her chest as he eased away from her. Even for a second, she shouldn't mourn the loss of his heat. His fingers brushed the line between her buttocks. She craved his touch. His love.

"Snake please…"

"Please what?"

"Fuck me!"

His cock nudged her sex. "This. Is this want you want, Sam?"

"Yes!" she screamed.

Ignoring her, he lifted her thigh and draped it over his forearm, spreading her wider.

"Mmm. You smell fucking fantastic." His tongue nibbled her ear.

"Damn you, Snake. Get off me or get in me!"

He grinned. "No problem. Nothing would make me happier, but we need a condom."

"Sod the condom. I'm on the pill and I'm clean." Hell, she hadn't been skin to skin with a man inside her for how long?

"Me too. Are you sure?"

"Never been surer." She turned her head and kissed him.

Mind-blowingly slow, he slid into her, stroked her insides until they found their mutual rhythm and gave into sensation. When his thrusts picked up the pace, she squeezed.

"Keep that up, and I'm not sure how long I'll last." A sharp tug pulled her closer. "I love you."

What the hell. Sam shook her head, her release building inside. She gulped for air. "No Snake don't love me. I can't give you what you want. God, Snake. Harder, please." *Make me come before I run.*

His hips slapped against her, giving her all she asked for. Spots of light danced across her vision and her orgasm ripped through her.

Snake tensed, one, two seconds before his roar bellowed in her ear. His semen flooded her insides, claiming everything she tried to keep from him. Her soul.

"Christ, Sam!"

Slowly, he turned her to face him. Butterfly kisses showered her forehead, eyelids, nose, and lips. He scared the shit out of her. She flicked her gaze over the walls, toward the ceiling, looking anywhere but at Snake.

He curled his fingers under her chin and brought her gaze level with his. "You with me? Come to bed."

"Let me go," she mumbled.

"No can do." He laid his chin on top of her head and sighed.

"I have to pee." She wiggled free and looked at him, prayed he'd read her mind and didn't ask awkward questions.

"I can hear you thinking, Sam. What's the matter? Not hard enough for you?"

She saw red at the anger in his voice. What gave him the right to be mad because she hadn't melted into his arms—returned three magic words?

"Tell me. What's wrong? Do you have a problem with caring?" His hand cupped her skull, refusing to let her glance away.

Her throat twisted into a big knot, making it difficult to speak. "It's not..." Sam struggled to find a reason he'd accept. "I don't need you to care."

"Too bad, Sam. That horse bolted. I care. A lot."

"Yes, well, get over yourself. Or someone will get hurt." Her laugh was forced. If anything had bolted, it was her heart. The moment Snake hadfirst kissed her, the damn muscle fled and stubbornly refused to return to the safety of the dark space in her chest.

"What are you afraid of, Sam?"

Nice one. Snake insisted on having the conversation that terrified her. She thrust her fists into his chest. "Let me go."

"Why? Let's talk. Share stuff," he asked.

She pushed harder and turned away, squeezing her eyes shut to trap the tears.

"Sam, please."

"No. I can't do this. Not tonight. I'll feed the dogs. You… er… go talk to Trigger."

"Fuck Trigger." Before Sam could pull away, Snake plunged for her mouth, sucking and nipping her lip, desperate to make her see they had a lifetime of stuff to share. An eternity to get to know each other.

He cursed his shit timing. Way to go. Tell the woman who means everything you love her when her friend's body is barely cold. That had to be it. The reason she couldn't look him in the eye.

Yes, he'd hoped she'd say she felt more than fucking lust for him. Sex with Sam. The best he'd ever had. But whenever she came apart in his arms, her eyes were full of more than physical pleasure. They brimmed with that indescribable something Knight and Doc swore black and blue had knocked them for six the moment they met their one and sodding only.

He wound his fingers in her hair. "Let me show you how much I care."

"I can't do this. I will hurt you."

Unable to make her do anything against her will, Snake released her, watched as she snatched on her underwear and jeans and willed himself the strength not to give up on them.

"I don't believe you would ever hurt me, Sam. Not that you don't have the power, but in my gut, I know you'd never use it."

"Maybe not intentionally." Her eyelashes flickered.

Christ. If anyone, he held the power to destroy. A fucking hypocrite encouraging Sam to lay herself bare when nothing had changed. He'd done as she'd said, weeks ago, and booked his flight to New York. Taken up Knight's job offer.

Sam mattered more to him than any woman he'd ever met. Always would. But being a protector, hunting down the bad guy, that was all he knew how to do, and he had no right to ask her for more.

"Snake?" Her fingers curled around his wrist. "Please understand."

He gripped her chin and brushed his lips over the top of her head. "Sam. There is something I need to tell you." Not the best time, but he'd run out of options.

"What is it?"

"Sit with me a sec." He sighed and placed his palm in the hollow of Sam's spine and coaxed her to the bed.

"I need to feed the dogs." Dinnertime suddenly important, she stepped further away from him.

"I know. It won't take a minute." He pulled up his pants and sat on the bed. At a safe distance because he refused to touch her, to insist she tear down her barriers just to satisfy his testosterone fed ego.

"Don't take it too hard, Snake. What do they say? It's me, not you."

Behind her forced smile, concern lurked in Sam's unshed tears, and, like the Tarzan she'd called him, he wanted to pound his chest, surround her with his arms, and shout, mine. He leant forward, elbows resting on his knees. Falling apart, he clasped his hands tight together and cleared his throat. "I'm leaving tomorrow. For New York."

"Right, of course. I wondered." Sam sniffed. "When will you be back? George is going to miss you. I will…" Her small gasp didn't escape his ears.

"Miss me? Don't." He couldn't bear to hear Sam say it, so he stopped her the only way he knew how. He came out fighting.

"Snake, I don't mean to upset you. If I could care for anyone, it would be you, but I don't have it in me. Not now. Not sure I ever will."

And this was when he should have walked off into the sunset. "Tell me." He reached for her hand, not wanting to risk her changing her mind.

CHAPTER THIRTY-TWO

Sam's fingers twitched beneath his palm. *No way, sweetheart.* Snake's gut churned, his head pounded, everything in him willing her to give in this one time and share whatever tormented her.

"Please, Sam." Okay, he was begging. He didn't give a fuck. He'd grovel on his knees if Sam trusted him with her secrets.

The slight softening in her body, the tentative step she took toward him, gave him hope. Energised, he stood and gently pulled her to him. "It'll be okay, sweetheart. I'm a big guy." The side of her cheek fluttered against his chest. A smile? "I can handle it, Sam. Tell me."

"I guess I should be over it by now. It didn't happen last week." Her voice came out small, muffled against his shirt.

Would he prefer it if she looked at him? You bet, but he stayed as still as he could, not wanting to interrupt.

"I was in love. Or at least, I thought I might be. Ed and I met in Afghanistan. Miserable, I enjoyed the way he made everyone laugh. Sounds dumb, but I found him magnetic, and I got sucked into his rainbow. He made living in hell bearable."

Tears dampened the front of his shirt. He'd give anything to lay her on the bed next to him and hold her for as long as it took until she believed him when he said everything would be okay. Again, he didn't move except to cup the back of Sam's neck and press her cheek deeper against his heart. "And…"

"We were coming back from helping out in a local village. I got mad because he threw up, kept throwing up, and I was torn between wanting to get him to base, possibly checked out by the medics, and making a stop at a local village to visit a kid I'd developed a soft spot for. Dumb, right? I decided to go for it, selfish, but we were leaving at the end of the week. Time had run out, and I'd promised."

Her sobs tore him apart, words barely making it through her tears. "Want to take a break, lie down for a bit?"

"No." Strong. He'd missed the mark.

"Okay, sorry, go on."

"Not much else to tell. Next ten minutes were a complete cluster-fuck. Ashad's mother went rogue with an assault rifle and a grenade." She sucked in a shaky breath. "Everyone died, mum, the kid, and Ed. All because I had to have my way."

His body shuddered with the horror Sam had gone through, held onto all this time. "It's not your fault, Sam. I don't have to be there to know Ashad's mum fell over the edge of something much bigger than you or I."

When she didn't respond, what could he say? He respected her too much to carry on with a string of cliché reassurances. Snake did the only thing his body and soul agreed upon. With the edge of his thumb, he tilted her chin until her eyes were level with his. "Open your eyes, sweetheart. Look at me." Sam's eyes fluttered open. *Score one for Snake.* "I love you."

His throat burned. Difficult to breathe as the deep ache in his chest threatened to split him in two. Had he witnessed terrible events during his time in service? Shit you couldn't offload, no matter how many shots of tequila you knocked back or shekels you paid the shrink? Yes. Like any other ex-service personnel.

He held her close, unable to speak, not daring to open his mouth in case he lost his resolve and promised her he'd spend the rest of his life with her only. She stayed silent, too, and raised her hands in between them and gently gave him a push. He let her go.

Honoured and humbled that Sam had trusted him, shared the horror haunting her, he wished the smile he couldn't wipe off his face when she kissed him, could convince her because words failed. They'd tried that.

He'd dropped his guard, told Sam he loved her, and she didn't feel the same. Or was it because she didn't believe he'd fill every day of her life with love? Fucked if he knew which.

His soul in shreds, he sucked in a deep breath and hardened his gaze. "I'll always be here for you, Sam. You need anything, say the word, and I will get to you whenever, wherever. I'll tell Knight to expect me in New York early next week so we can deal with the cops and make arrangements for Jim. Trigger will stay after I'm gone. You're Sentinel family. He'll protect you with his life."

"I guess this is it, then." Sam's chest rose and fell with a deep sigh that matched his own.

He missed her already but wouldn't cave or push her further.

"Thanks, John. Will George go with you or stay here?"

"If it's okay with you and Bounce? I'll send for him when I'm settled."

"Sure. Don't forget to mail us a postcard from the Empire State Building. That's the Big Apple classic, right? For George. I'll pin it on the wall of the new kennels."

George hauled his rear end from the wooden floor, refused to look at Snake, and whimpered.

"Well, sun's up. Best start work. Bit late, but do you think you could add fixing the cameras to your job list?" Sam's half smile felt like a slap to his face.

The side of his eye twitched. *Hell no.* "Leave it to me." He tightened his fists and swallowed the rock in his throat.

Sam brushed the hair from his forehead. "Thanks. I'll go find Trigger. He can help me assess what's left of the barn. I haven't had the heart to look since the fire. Probably nothing much worth saving."

"Sure. Whatever you need."

"Okay, then. See you around one for lunch." Sam kicked the door open for him. "I hope you and Trigger are okay with leftovers." She cupped George's cheeks and nuzzled his nose.

Jealous of a feckin' dog. He left, hating that he cared.

Sam braced against the kitchen bench as the simple task of preparing a cup of tea made her stomach roll. Bounce nudged her wet snout between the fingers of her spare hand.

"Don't be pushy, girl. I'm getting there," she snapped. Bounce turned to George, enlisting his help. Together, they nudged and licked until she had no option but to stop shuffling cups and pay them attention, thank them for being right there by her side.

Part of her was glad she'd cleared the air with Snake. Her heart ached every time she imagined him at the airport waiting to catch his plane. After Ed, building a fortress around her heart had been no big deal until John walked through her damn door, after which living behind barriers became much more difficult. He chipped away at every crack in her walls.

Last night had been no different than most. Lost in nonsense dreams. Stray dogs in rooftop forests, chased by a man with a box of matches, toppled over the edge. John forever around the next corner. *I love you.* Somewhere out there, she heard him but never found him. And each time she woke, her feet were cold blocks of ice weighing her down.

Fresh air called before the what-ifs smothered her. Fixing the barn would be an extra drain on her dwindling cash flow, and the outhouse had to go. How could she look at another fridge and not think of Jim? She couldn't change what had happened, but as she'd told the police, she was damn sure it had to be Baxter fucking with her life. Jenna hadn't seen him since the night of the fire. The best thing, Jenna had finally come to her senses and they both hoped he'd never show himself again.

Blinded by tears, a quick swipe with her sleeve handling her drippy nose, Sam opened the door and called out to Trigger. Her heart jumped when she saw the enormous bunch of flowers on the wrought-iron table. She crooked her head to the side, half-expecting Snake's face to pop around the corner. His eyes on track for the familiar roam over her body before he devoured her in a kiss. *No.* She closed her eyes and cursed the thought.

Thank the stars George had it together. His bark forced her feet to the ground. A large black thumbprint tagged the edge of the slanted envelope hanging from the bright red ribbon holding the tissue paper around the bouquet in place. Not Snake's style. Sam hesitated, allowed herself a chuckle, dismissed her heart's misstep, and tore open the envelope.

You have my property. Follow these instructions and bring me the bag. Tell no one. Keep lover boy out of it. I see him or the cops, and Tom will suffer before I slit his throat.

CHAPTER THIRTY-THREE

Snow thumped the window and stuck in odd shapes to the glass before sliding defeated onto the sill. Her body clock, set to sparrow fart in the military, never reset to lazing in bed in civilian life.

Sam's fingers stayed tucked under the sheet while she listened to Snake snore in the spare room. The last time he would sleep at her place before he left for New York. Her palms itched, tempted to slip under his blanket and roam freely over his body. But that wouldn't be fair to either of them.

Struggling not to say anything either might regret, they'd had their tense moments the past week. She'd miss him, but not his snoring. Like all his Sentinel buddies, John slept light. Afraid to wake him, Sam inched her body from under the sheets, grabbed her clothes, tucked her boots under her arm, and tiptoed out of her bedroom. Grabbing her rucksack and a pair of socks, she checked her phone.

Baxter's messages had escalated beyond desperate. Any second, he could completely lose the plot, and that scared her. It had taken longer than it should have to find his damn toolbox. It made her mad to think if only she hadn't fussed over where to put the silos, Baxter would have his shit and be a million miles away. Jim's murder—another death on her hands.

With Baxter's directions seared into her brain, she shoved her uncombed hair under her hat and went to fix Trigger coffee. John's insistence on leaving Trigger as bodyguard irritated, but she didn't argue. After he left, she'd let Knight know Trigger didn't need to stay.

Stationed outside in John's Jeep, Trigger would have to be dead not to notice her leave. As she didn't plan on putting a bullet in his brain, she laced his drink with the sleeping pills they'd prescribed for her at the hospital. She would apologise later, but for now, Baxter's deadline loomed.

She flipped the latch on the door and left, grateful for the company of the moon pushing through the clouds, a few stars struggling to shine. Eyes closed, one hand resting on the holster on the passenger seat beside him, a stranger might believe Trigger slept. Sam knew better.

He turned before she tapped and rolled down his window. The glint in his eye said he'd been hanging out for the mug of caffeine.

"Hey, you're up late. Everything, okay?" He turned around to look back at the house. "Where's Snake?"

"Back in the house. I couldn't sleep, but..." She gave a few snorts. Trigger cracked up, obviously used to John's nocturnal noises. "Thought you might like some coffee?"

"Won't say no. You're an angel. Thanks."

The mug sprang from her hands to his lips. *Fantastic.* "Enjoy. I'll see you at breakfast."

"Definitely. I'm hanging out for a bacon sarnie, but this will keep me going until then."

"You're welcome. 'Night." As she turned towards the house, the moon played its part and disappeared behind a cloud. Under the darkness, she wove around the back and into the trees. One last check of the Jeep to make sure Trigger hadn't seen her.

Apart from an owl hooting and the wind burning her cheeks, nothing else disturbed the night. Soon it would be light. She had to get moving if she hoped to put miles between her and the kennels before John woke and realised she had gone. He would not be happy. Would he follow? Doubtful. She grinned. Most likely, he'd throw his hands in the air, finally give up on her, and head for the airport. No less than she deserved.

Distracted, she didn't see the patch of black ice. One hand struck out, searching for anything to stop her fall, and found a low branch. Luckily it held. Pulling the hood of her jacket firmly over her head, Sam slipped further into the cover of the trees and headed across the fields to Jenna's. Her friend kept the key under the wheel of the old station wagon in her shed. A sense of dread swept over her as she pulled the cover off the vehicle. What if Jenna had moved the key? Luckily, no. She opened the door, climbed in and started the engine. She expected the lights to come on in Jenna's house, but the inside stayed dark.

Hands firmly wrapped around the steering wheel, she drove fast along the narrow road, occasionally checking the mirror to make sure no one followed. Despite the heater blowing full blast, her hands stayed cold. Terrified. Could she do this? A long time had passed since there'd been any need to use her military skills.

It irked to admit it, but she'd be a lot more confident if John had her back. But he had much bigger things to worry about. She cracked open the window and sucked in the bitter air. All week, she'd been on the brink of confessing how much she loved him, but heading up Sentinel in New York fit him perfectly. John would always be happiest shielding and protecting others. Not playing happy kennel mate with her in the Yorkshire Dales.

Her phone vibrated in her pocket. Jenna? Ready to fess up to pinching her car, Sam's thumb hovered over the green button. Ahead, bright lights breached the horizon before a beat-up black sedan crested the small hill and rolled to a stop a few feet from her. She tossed her phone on the seat and waited. The doors stayed closed.

What the hell is Baxter playing at? Fuck him. She didn't need his crap mind games. Slowly, she released the lock, nudged open the door with her boot, and stepped out into the glare of his headlights. Too late. It crossed her mind that the next thing might be a bullet hitting her chest.

Easy. No sudden movement. Baxter might be madder than a wet hen, but the chances of him making a wrong move before he had the box hidden under her rear seat were slim.

"You better be alone," he shouted as he stepped from his car, clutching a pistol.

Sam shaded her eyes from the bright light. "Look around." A quick twirl on her heel didn't serve any real purpose except to give her a moment to take a breath. "I'm alone."

"Smart woman. Guess I didn't need my insurance after all."

"Cut the crap, Baxter. Let's get this over with."

"Don't be nasty, Sam. I have someone here who's keen to talk to you. Tom, say hello to Aunty Sam." Baxter's hiss rose like steam into the icy air. "Now where's my property?"

"Tom. Everything is going to be all right. Are you okay?" She forced her voice not to shake but doubted she succeeded. Jenna must be going insane. "You can have it as soon as I'm sure the boy is unhurt."

"Don't listen to him Sam, he has a…"

"Shut your face," a voice from inside the vehicle said. Baxter hadn't come alone. A loud crack. Tom moaned.

"You touch him again and you'll never get what you came for. Hang in there, Tom. We'll be home for breakfast." Sam curled her hands into tight fists. If, make that when, she got her hands on this piece of dog meat, his smirk wouldn't be the only thing he'd lose.

"Oh, please. You're breaking my heart. Now give me my stuff," Baxter yelled.

"On the back seat. Let's trade? You get it and Tom comes with me."

"Fine. Don't try anything, and if I see your fuck buddy, Tommy dies first."

"I told you. No one is with me." The way the twat waved his weapon around made her very nervous.

"Get out of the car, kid." Baxter grabbed Tom's ear and yanked him out of the vehicle.

Heart in her throat, Sam froze, didn't dare move, as Tom staggered and did his best to stay upright. The bastard had beaten him, torn his clothes, and a deep gash slashed close to his eye. "What did you do to him, you piece of shit?" Sam roared, praying Baxter's twisted mind hadn't stretched past the beating.

"The kid has a mouth on him. Never knows when to shut the fuck up, so I shared a few pointers."

"You bastard, I am going to—"

"Nothing. You will do sweet fuck all. Now, hand it over before I lose my patience." Baxter pulled Tom into his side, pointed the pistol at his temple, and strode towards her.

Almost level, he thrust the boy into her arms. Tom fell against her, his thin arms clutching his torso. He gulped hard, trying not to cry. She wanted to hug him, check his injuries, but daren't. She had to keep both hands free. "I'm sorry. I promise this will all be over soon." Closing her eyes, she willed herself to stay in control, not to lose it and get them both killed.

She opened them again in time to see Baxter grab his bag and charge them. She pushed Tom out of his way but didn't have time to brace for a fight. He grabbed Tom's neck and snatched her elbow, his filthy fingernails digging into her forearm as he dragged them to his car.

"Get your hands off me. You've got what you want. Don't make things worse."

"Yes. Thank you, but you understand I can't afford to leave any loose ends." The nuzzle of his gun poked her ribs. "Dogs get put down when they have no further use. Nothing new, ay, Sam?"

"Okay. Take me. Leave the boy. Please," she begged. "He has nothing to do with this." Like Ashad—a victim of crazy adults.

Baxter switched positions and aimed his weapon at Tom. "No witnesses."

"Please."

"What do you care? This kid's nothing to you. Shut up and get in the car." Baxter cackled.

"Where are we going?" Tom whimpered.

"Somewhere they will never find you. Now get the fuck in the car before I kill you both and leave you for your boyfriend to find."

Tom shuddered. It broke her heart watching him try his best to be brave. "It's okay, mate. Hop in. I'm right here. I won't let him hurt you." She glared at Baxter. Her gut churned, more with anticipation than fear. No matter what it took, she'd kill this animal.

"Get in." Baxter opened the back door and passed his gun to the man sitting in the front of the car. "Get out. I want you in the back with them. They make one move, shoot."

The stranger nodded, smiled, and did as Baxter asked. He sat between her and Tom. Baxter started the engine and tore off at speed. Tires squealed. The car jerked forward, throwing her hard against the car door. Tom cried out. She squeezed his hand, trying to reassure him. If it cost Sam life, she'd make sure he got home to Jenna.

The man sitting between them and chuckled. At what she didn't know, but in her peripheral vision, something glistened before she felt the sharp sting in her neck and her breath caught in her chest. Tom wriggled, trying to avoid the prick from another syringe. She tried to stop him, but her arms were dead weight, and she was falling, faster, deeper into the darkness at the edge of her vision.

"Morning." Baxter tore the dirty rag from her face.

Sam winced at the sudden rip and burn searing her face. The foul stench of sweat and alcohol assaulting her nose made her vomit. The response earned her a swift backhand from Baxter, who didn't appreciate the spew on his boot. Her head jerked at an awkward angle and stars shot across her vision.

Another smack knocked her to the floor. Every nerve in her body screamed, but she refused to make a sound as her shoulder broke the fall. Teeth slammed down on her tongue and the rusty taste of blood flooded her mouth.

Light filtering through the broken shutters landed on Tom. He lay unmoving in the corner. Sam called to him, but his name came out wrong. The edge of her tongue pressed uncomfortably against her swollen lips. Snot and blood streamed from her nose.

Ignoring the pixies slinging sledgehammers at her head, she tried to sit, but Baxter's boot landed on her arse, kicking her closer to Tom. By the time she scrambled to her knees, the bastard had gone. She swallowed the blood trickling from her nose into her throat. "Hey. Wake up, buddy." Tendrils of matted hair covered Tom's eyes. "Come on, talk to me. Wake up." She shook him until he groaned.

Thank God. Tears welled in her eyes, threatening to suck the last of her courage. "That's it. Sit up. Let me look at you."

"Sam, I can't..."

She stroked his cheek, but held off on the promise his hero, Snake, would come for him, even as her heart reached for John. "Sit up. We have to find a way out of here before Baxter comes back. That's it. Good lad." She stroked the hair from his eyes.

Not if, but when they got out of there, Sam swore she'd make this up to Tom ten times over, play FIFA any time he asked. First, they had to survive.

Damn. The door rattled and Baxter and the other man strode into the room, murder written all over their shitty faces. "You've got what you wanted. What do you plan on doing with us?"

"Shut up, bitch." Another slap sent pain spiralling from her head to her toes. Sam struck out with her elbow, banking on the slim chance she'd reach his gut. No way, but it felt great to try. His buddy slapped her hard. This time she stayed still and swore to fight another day.

CHAPTER THIRTY-FOUR

Snake woke with a start and immediately reached for the warm body he wished he had pressed to his side. Oh yeah, separate beds. Not really what his head or his blue balls appreciated, but if nothing else, his various foster families had knocked the gentleman into him.

One more day and he'd be gone. He tumbled out of the cold sheets and crept the short distance to Sam's room. If she still slept, he didn't want to wake her. Every morning this past week, he'd worked hard to convince her to take it easy, spoilt her with breakfast. Nothing less than she deserved, even if being close to her stretched his control.

"Sam?" It took less than a second to see the empty bed. He patted the sheets. Cold. Heart in throat, he checked the bathroom, guessing before he opened the door that Sam had gone. George, Bounce right behind him, watched him intently as he pulled on his pants and shirt. Grabbing his coat. Dressing took longer than usual. Slow motion as his brain worked overtime. He shoved on his boots and tore outside.

Bounce whimpered. Why hadn't Sam taken her dog? Peering at the dawn, he finally admitted his world had gone to shit.

Out front, Trigger sat with his head resting awkwardly against the window. Feet hardly touching the ground, Snake rushed to his Jeep and pulled on the door. It didn't budge. "Trig. Wake up, man. Where's Sam?" His fist beat the window.

"Huh?" Bleary-eyed, Trigger swallowed and shook his head.

"Sam, where's Sam?" Snake shouted.

"Inside. With you."

"She's gone."

Bounce barked. Refused to stop.

"Bollocks. I must have fallen asleep." Trigger scrubbed his face and opened his door.

None of them ever fell asleep on the job. An upturned mug sat on the seat next to his teammate. Snake lifted it to his nose. "Bloody hell, man. She drugged you."

Reaching inside the vehicle, he flung Trigger's arm around his shoulder, helped him into the house, took out his phone, and called Knight.

"It's the middle of the night, man. What's up?" Knight grumbled.

"Sam's gone." He leaned against the wall and scrubbed his chin. Anger, mostly fear, screwed with his gut. He should have known Sam would get fed up waiting for Baxter to surface.

"Where the hell is Trigger?" Knight asked.

"Hovering in the doorway. Sam drugged him. I'm going after her, but he needs medical attention."

"N... no. I'm fine. Don't need the hospital." Trigger stuttered and waved his hand.

"For Christ's sake, you're making me seasick, swaying around like that. Sit your arse down for a sec."

"Snake. What do you need?" Knight asked.

"Not sure. First, I have to figure out where she's gone. I'll be in touch."

"Roger that. I'll contact Spanner and Doc," Knight confirmed. He didn't need to ask. "Hang in there. I'll tell you when we're close. Keep us up to speed."

Snake hung up, tossed his phone on the table, and rammed his fist into the wall. He didn't have a clue where to look for Sam, so he ignored the blast of pain and slammed it again.

"Give it a rest, man. Think of my fucking head if you don't give a shit about your hand."

"Piss off," Snake snarled and steadied himself against the door frame. Trigger had a point. He'd be no use to Sam with a broken hand. "Sorry, man."

Apologies were cheap, but his mate chuckled and pinched between his eyebrows. Probably the headache from hell making him wince. Snake went to the sink to fetch him some water.

"What's that?" Trigger asked, pointing at the small piece of paper lying on the ground beside the fridge.

He wasn't in the mood to tidy up after Sneaky Sam, but he scraped it off the floor and reeled from the blast of relief flooding his system. A soddin' map shivered in his trembling hand. It wasn't much, and he couldn't be sure that was where Sam was headed, but they had nothing else. She might be heading into a trap, and he sure as hell wasn't hanging around for the bad news. He turned to Trigger. "I'm going after her. How are you doing? Think you can bring Knight up to speed while I drive?"

"Getting better. Let's go."

Snake grabbed the keys from Trigger and called to the dogs. Seconds later, they were on the road. He drove as fast as he could through the slush, turned to ice overnight, making the road treacherous. Life without Sam meant no life. Pity he hadn't worked harder to show her.

He glanced at his watch, praying they got to her on time. He grabbed the ringing phone from his pocket, expecting the boss to demand an update, one he didn't have. Instead, Sam's smiling face stared at him. No way. What were the fucking chances she'd come to her bloody senses? He put the phone on speaker.

"Hello." Nothing. "Sam, where are you?" And then it hit him. Her fear, like smoke, drifted over the phone.

"Good evening."

Not Sam, but Snake knew damn well who answered.

"Who's this?" he asked, keeping his tone even.

"Baxter. Remember me? Of course, you do. Your girl's with me. Like a word?"

"Put her on, fucker. If you've hurt her., I'll tear your heart from your chest and feed it to…" So much for not wanting to spook the fucker.

"John?" she asked, her voice shaky.

"Right here. Are you okay?"

"Fine. He wants you to come. Snake. He has Tom."

"I found his map. I'm on my way."

"Brilliant. Don't take too long, hero. I have a short attention span. Let's say fifteen minutes. I may get bored if you take any longer and have to entertain myself." Baxter laughed.

"Don't you fucking touch her. Either of them." The phone went dead.

"Let's end this tosser," Trigger said, struggling to stay conscious.

And that was why Snake had picked him for his 2IC in New York. Never give up should be tattooed across his forehead. The flashing light on the dashboard caught his eye. The petrol gauge hovered on empty. Vaguely, he remembered Sam reminding him to fill his tank. Clutching the steering wheel, he commanded the pile of junk to keep moving. A few more miles, almost there, when his phone rang again.

"Are you here, or should I let the games begin?" Baxter said.

"Keep your shirt on, sunshine. I'm here. Dying to catch up." He tapped Trigger's shoulder, signalling for him to pull his shit together.

"We're in the cabin at the end of the drive. Hurry."

Destination reached, Snake pulled over and opened his door, then let out the dogs. "Call Knight. Let him know where we are. George, with me, Come."

"Wait for me," Trigger insisted.

"Appreciate it, but in your state, you're more of a liability than a help."

A single nod. Not happy, but his teammate acknowledged his order.

Armed with his bare hands, his favourite weapon, Snake ran along the path and hammered on the cabin door. No answer. His pulse kicked up, adrenaline coursing through him. He thumped again, shifted to the side, and kicked the door open. No gunfire, no ambush, so he pressed on, planting a cautious step inside the cabin. It smelled of mildew, dust, and burnt wood. "Sam? Can you hear me? Talk to me."

"Up here, hero." Baxter peered over the loft railing above them. His arm was hooked firmly around Sam's neck.

Figuring Baxter could have picked him off any time, he took the steps several at a time. A bare bulb illuminated the cavity. Snake's foot hit the top step and Baxter loomed in front of him. A large hunting knife lay across Sam's throat. To his left, a man he'd never seen before held Tom, his hand clamped over the lad's mouth.

"Generous of you to join us." He waved the knife and Sam's breath hitched. "Stand over there."

"You shouldn't have come." Sam glared at him.

He rolled his eyes. "Nearly didn't. Plane to catch and all that."

"Trigger. Is he okay?" she asked.

"Aside from the headache from hell, he's peachy. You've looked better."

Baxter stared at them as though they'd lost it. He might be right. The bruises on Sam's face made him want to dive for the fuckhead, but he wouldn't risk all their lives. Their gazes locked. Sam's unsaid command—do nothing. In that moment, he couldn't figure out who was doing the saving. Afraid he'd take his chances if he looked at her scared face any longer, he fixed his attention on Baxter. "What the fuck do you want?"

"The last piece of my puzzle to fall into place. I figure your three dead bodies will complete the perfect picture. Almost, there's still Jenna," he snarled, obviously enjoying Tom's terrified whimpers.

Snake took a step towards him. "Take it easy, Baxter. No one need die. The police are on their way. If I were you, I'd get as far away from here as I could, while I still had time."

"Shut the hell up." Baxter swiped the air between them with his knife.

Snake jumped to avoid the blade.

"Leave them alone. It's me who screwed with your plans. Let them go," Sam roared.

Blood pounded in Snake's head. Terrified she'd keep struggling and get her throat cut, Snake put his finger to his lips, silently begging her, just this once, to stop speaking. "Sam. Look at me. Knight, the police, they're coming."

"Yeah, so is Christmas." Baxter rocked and swayed, his shoulders heaving with laughter he struggled to keep in check.

CHAPTER THIRTY-FIVE

Snake hurled his full body weight into Baxter. They crashed in a tangled heap, air exploding from their lungs. Bells rang, stars spun in a mad circle above him, and Snake's vision dimmed. Far away, he heard George bark, waiting for his command.

Baxter recovered first and threw a right hook. Snake swerved to avoid the punch, failed. The next time, he blocked and shoved Baxter off him. Crazy mad, the bastard kept coming. Breathing hard, Snake found his balance and bounced on the balls of his feet, waiting for Baxter to make his next move. The guy was big, but no match for his skill level, despite the lucky punches. Rage blazed in the fucker's eyes. No problem. On the same sodding page there.

"Bring it, prick. Let's get this done. I have places to be." He flicked his fingers, egging the arsehole to him. Snake's next punch hit its target.

Baxter's head flew sideways, blood spraying from his nose, as he threw another punch and landed a lucky kick to Snake's ribs. His body had taken worse, but sensing victory, Baxter lurched for Sam. *Not happening.* Snake tucked his chin to his chest and charged again, pounding his fists into Baxter's torso. Blood trickling from a cut above his eye made it difficult to see clearly, but the sweet crack of bone brought on a smile.

"Kill him!" Baxter screamed at the man holding Tom.

Snake pivoted and saw Sam already grappling for the knife in the guy's hand.

But the distraction cost him. A blow to the top of his head sent Snake crashing to his knees. Sam's scream reverberated in the loft space. He'd failed to protect them.

Sam hesitated. She couldn't let anyone hurt Tom, but Snake lay unconscious. Or worse. Terrified he might be dead, she swung her fist full force and belted Baxter's partner in the mouth. Gobsmacked by the move, he brought his hand to his jaw and stared at her in disbelief.

"George. Attack," Sam yelled at Snake's dog, and legs wide, she braced for a second round.

George snarled and launched at Tom's attacker, bit his bottom leg, and held. The guy howled, rocked a few times, and crumbled. "Tom, to me. George, release, come." Tom flew into her arms, George limping behind him.

"Enough, bitch. Hold it right there." One arm clutching his belly, Baxter hauled himself to his feet. Bent double, he flipped the safety on his weapon.

"Okay, okay. Take it easy." She raised her hands in surrender.

"Outside, bitch, and don't try anything. I'm done with you. You're dead," he cackled. "But I'm a fair man. You have a choice. Die here or live to smell the fresh air an hour longer. Which is it?"

Sam didn't waste time wondering what twisted mind considered she had options. "Anything you say. Just don't hurt the boy."

"Not this again. Move. *All* of you." Baxter waved the gun at the man nursing his mangled leg.

He grunted and looked at Sam. "Huh?"

"Search me, mate." Sam shook her head, equally confused why he'd lobbed numb nuts in with her and Tom.

"Why is it every other guy I employ… Sons of bitches. Every one of them turns out to be a fucking idiot," Baxter whined, waved his gun at the exit, and hissed. "Go on, dick, with the others."

Yes. Baxter's ribs were killing him. That lifted her spirits until she flicked a look in John's direction. Eyes closed, he didn't twitch. He'd said the police were on their way. Where the hell were they? *I love you,* she mouthed silently. Snake had come for them. If it got him killed, she'd never be able to live with herself.

"Snake. Goddamit, wake up, man. Snake…"

"Okay, okay. Keep your hands to yourself." Snake shoved Trigger's mitt from his face and swore, mortified Baxter had gotten the upper hand and that it may have cost Sam and Tom their lives. "Where are they?" He grabbed Trigger's shirt and hoisted himself upright.

"Easy. They took off a few minutes ago. Can you stand?"

With Trigger's help, he clambered to his feet. "Yeah. Let's go. Where's George?"

"They left him. He's back in the Jeep with Bounce. As soon as she saw Sam and the boy, I thought she'd claw a hole in the roof. Anything to get to her."

Snake nodded and huffed. That did not surprise him.

With each step, the world became less hazy, and by the time they reached the vehicle, his head had cleared sufficiently to drive. George poked his nose over his seat. "Okay, boy. We'll find them. Look after your mate." He raised an arm and scrubbed George's ears, and aimed his snout toward Bounce, whose claws tap-danced on the back seat. "Trig. Which way?

"That way." Trigger nodded to the left.

Car in gear, wipers working overtime to clear the mud and slush splattering the windscreen, they tore after Sam and Tom. Just when Snake thought they'd lost them, he crested a small hill and Baxter's vehicle swung into view. "There."

Snake slammed his foot on the accelerator, giving the Jeep as much power as it would take, but the shit conditions hampered their speed. Tyres squealed as he fought to stay on the road.

"Slow down," Trigger said.

His brain offered a salute to that fucking great idea while his heart sprinted after Sam. "Hang on." For a split second, he thought of the dogs loose in the back and prayed they were okay. Neither he nor Trigger carried guns. They were illegal in the UK. No head-out-the-window shooting in England's country lanes. Bare hands, their primary weapon. And if he guessed rightly, they both had regulation knife strapped to their ankles.

He pumped the accelerator again, hoping to hell they had enough petrol in the tank. Once they got ahead of Baxter, he would create some sort of diversion to make him stop. *Then you're mine.*

"This guy's fucking crazy," Trigger muttered. "Knob'ed keeps this up and he'll take us all off the soddin' road."

Not what Snake needed to hear considering his heart had skipped way too many beats trying to picture a scenario where this ended well. He gripped the steering wheel and willed the Jeep to stay in a straight line. The dogs whined and scrambled on the back seat.

"Christ. Son of a..." Trigger grabbed the strap above his head and slammed his foot onto a non-existent brake.

Time stood still as Baxter's car swerved on a patch of black ice, spun several times, and careered off the road. Captured by momentum, out of control, it bounced over the field, rolled, and slammed into a tree. "No!"

"Fuck me." Trigger whistled.

Wind howled through the trees. The vehicle rocked and groaned, smoke billowing from the bonnet. Windows exploded and the rear doors burst open. And all Snake could do was watch as he slammed to a halt at the side of the road and lurched from the Jeep.

Reaching Sam his prime objective, Snake planted one hand on the fence post to steady himself, vaulted over it, and swallowed the bile rising in his throat. He refused to listen to the demon in his head, the one insisting no one could have survived. Right behind him Trigger, dialled 999 before contacting Knight.

Focussed. Drawing on the power of his long legs, Snake ploughed through the snow. "Sam?" His voice, riddled with terror, didn't pass a whisper. Not even in action, facing heavy enemy fire, had he ever been this terrified.

Baxter's car lay on its side, the front end destroyed. Flames, fast eating their way to the passengers in the front, shot from the engine.

"It's going to blow." Trigger gripped his arm, trying to pull him away from the smoking vehicle.

They didn't have time to wait, it could explode at any minute. Snake wrenched out of Trigger's grip, jumped on the rear bumper, climbed across the boot, and seized the rear door handle. "Fuck." Jammed. He planted his foot firmly on the frame and pulled with everything in him.

Sam opened her eyes and began frantically pounding on the window.

"Hang on," he cried, but the door wouldn't budge.

"Get Tom," she mouthed.

Furious at the resignation on her face, he thumped the window. "Don't you give up on me."

As if the day could get any worse, another gust of wind egged the fire closer to the petrol tank. Heart pounding, Snake hammered on the glass. "You hear me. I'm going to get you out. Can you open it from the inside?"

Sam shook her head. And fuck him if she didn't smile. "Tom. Get Tom."

"Here, try this." Trigger handed him a small tree branch.

Snake wedged it in between the frame and door. A creak and a slight bend were all he needed. He tossed the branch on the ground, tore at the metal until his fingertips bled, and it wedged open enough for him to reach Sam.

"Tom first." Sam batted his hand, leaned against her seat, and made space for Tom to wriggle in front of her.

"Okay. To me, Tom." He grabbed the lad and handed him over the edge to Trigger. "You got him?"

"Yeah. Safe," Trigger confirmed.

"Now you. Let's get the fuck out of here."

"What about Baxter?"

Dead for all he cared. "They're both gone. Out you come." He flipped the seatbelt lock and dragged Sam into his arms. Battered and bleeding, but alive. Relief roared through him.

"Tom?" Sam swayed on her feet.

"Trigger has him."

One hand round her waist, he drew her into his side, and they stumbled forward. Too bad they hadn't made it further before the car exploded. The force of the blast threw them flat. Sparks rained around them.

CHAPTER THIRTY-SIX

Sam opened her eyes. Every muscle ached, and when large hands tried to stop her from sitting, she groaned in protest.

The car had crashed, an explosion. "Tom. Oh, God. Where is he?

"Take it easy. It's me, Snake. Lie still. Let Doc look at you." Snake gently placed his palm on her chest to stop her from jumping up to find the lad.

She couldn't hear him properly, his deep voice muffled by the ringing in her ears. "Where's Tom?" she demanded.

"In the spare room. Kate's with him. He's fine. Jenna's on her way," he shouted.

"Take me to him."

"Not until Doc gives you the all-clear."

"Now, Snake. Or so help me, I will…"

Heaving a sigh, he lifted her off the sofa. Biting her lip to stifle a sob, she lassoed his neck and held on tight. "Baxter? You sure he's…" she had to ask.

"Dead."

The first piece of positive news she'd heard in too long.

Snake laid another blanket over Sam and tucked the edges around her legs. It had been almost a week since the accident, and she'd been so quiet it scared him. He wanted the old Sam, the one that drove him crazy, fought with him until he craved make-up sex.

Doc stood in the doorway, a smug smile on his face. A true mate, he and Kate had hung around in Giggleswick and visited twice a day to check on Sam, tend the angry cuts and bruises covering her body. He'd never stop wishing Baxter had lived so he could kill him with his bare hands.

"Thanks, Doc. You're sure she's okay?" He'd asked a hundred times. And he'd ask a hundred more.

"I'm sure. Stop worrying before you have a fucking coronary, and we never get home. Sam has nine lives. Keep her comfortable, make sure she eats something with her medication, and we'll be here tomorrow."

"Expect a party," Kate added. "I hear Lily's on her way."

"I get the picture. Do you think you could ask Lily to give it a couple of days?" A selfish prick, he wanted Sam to himself until he left for New York the day after tomorrow. Then Lily could step up and look after Sam.

"Can't promise, but I'll try." Kate smiled. The pressure of her arm on his shoulder brought the lump back to his throat.

"Come on, Nurse Kate, I have some doctorly duties I need help with," Doc said.

"Mmm. Sounds interesting," Kate purred. "Bye, Snake, see you tomorrow."

Snake's watch pinged. A reminder the police were due in an hour. Same cops. More questions. They'd been up, down, and around the same information more than once. Exhausted, Sam repeated everything she knew about Baxter and the drugs.

"John."

"That's me." He turned to the sofa, but Sam's eyes were closed, her nose perched on the edge of the blanket. She often said his name, but nothing followed, as if she just wanted to confirm he existed. He'd gladly do whatever she needed to make damn sure she understood he was no fucking illusion. Flesh and blood with a heart that wished things were different, that she'd join him in New York.

He bent and kissed her forehead. Ten minutes before he needed to wake her. He hummed the song he'd heard her sing in the shower until the cops pulled up outside. "Hey, Sam. Wake up, sweetheart. The cops are here. I can send them away if you want to sleep some more."

"No, it's okay." Her voice sounded hoarse, tired. "I want to get this over with, so I can move on and get back to my life. I'm sure you need this to be over, too."

"Not soon enough." He winked, hoping to make her smile. Only one woman claimed him like no other, but she never hinted at feeling the same. For the best. He'd escape to New York. Free his headspace.

Ten minutes before boarding. Snake drank the last of his beer, pulled out his phone, and tried Sam again. One last chance. *Come on, sweetheart. Pick up.* Since leaving the kennels, he had tried to call her a dozen times, but she never answered. Unlike him, Sam wasn't umbilically tied to her mobile.

He should have tried harder, took longer to say a proper goodbye. There were other planes, for Christ's sake. Maybe he could have convinced her their time together had been much more than sex, that he wasn't Ed. But did it matter? Sam said she didn't love him. Oh, sure, in another life, another time crap, she might, big might, care for him. No use pretending a long-distance relationship could work for either of them.

"This is the last call for passengers on Delta flight DL5997 to New York. Mr John Smith, if you are in the terminal, please go to gate thirty-five, where your flight is preparing for immediate take-off."

Snake tossed his bag over his shoulder and tried one more time to reach Sam. Knight had called him on Sunday, concerned he'd missed his farewell drinks. He made some dumb excuse. A hitch with a new team member. The boss didn't believe him—who cared? One more drink, one more best-of-luck slap on the back, and he'd have cracked. Told Knight to find someone else.

"Delta flight DL5997 to New York is closed..." He should have started running, not felt relieved that he might miss his flight, but he slowed his pace, turned on his heel and headed to the luggage area to claim his offloaded bags. He'd call Knight, throw him another line of bullshit, hope he didn't kick his arse out of Sentinel, and book a later flight. He had to do this. One last shot. Convince Sam to give him, them, a chance. As slow as she needed, until she came around to his way of thinking, loving.

Lily would know where to find Sam. He stepped out of the terminal and hailed a cab. Unfortunately for him, his love life didn't rate on the boss' busy agenda.

"What the fuck is going on, Snake?" Knight stood outside his building, glowering at him as he stepped out of the cab.

"Slight detour, boss."

"Say again. Your arse should be hovering over the ocean halfway to New York."

"Yeah, yeah, but I have to speak with Lily first."

"What the hell does my wife have to do with this?" Knight tossed his hand in the air.

Taking advantage of the slight turn in the boss' body, Snake dodged past and headed for the lift.

Girls stuck together, and Snake used to swear nothing could be as strong as the guy thing, the unbreakable male bond, but Lily's walls were made of reinforced concrete. In the end, the boss lost it and threw him out of their flat, insisting he get his intel from someone other than his wife.

Jenna had been the same when he rang. Tight-lipped. Had no idea where Sam had taken herself off to recoup. If only the dogs could talk. Eventually, when he hinted a ring might feature in his plans, Kate, the card-carrying matchmaker, caved.

A sodding camping trip? Whatever happened to a weekend at a spa? Pampering, candles, painted toenails? He hired a car and headed further north. Scotland. Even colder than the Dales. A blizzard accompanied him all the way up the motorway.

By the time he arrived the camp site reception was closed for the night. Wait until morning, the polite thing to do, but he'd left his manners with the fried egg sandwich at the truck stop twenty miles away.

He raised a fist, thumped on the office door, and considered he'd caught his first break in shit knew how long when it creaked open. A short, bald, bloke who, judging by the way he squinted, had left his glasses by the bed, growled at him.

"Can't you read, laddie? We're closed. Come back in the morning."

Snake shoved his foot in the door before the Scot could slam it in his face. "Sorry to disturb you, but it's important. I need to find Sam Leigh. I believe she's camping here. Please, point me in the direction of her site and I'll let you get some sleep."

"So important it couldn't wait until morning?"

"Yes."

"*Dinnae* see the sign? There are opening times for a reason. We toned our sleep so we can get up early and deal with those keen to be leaving and on their way."

"I apologise. But it's a matter of life and death." A stretch, but he didn't have a lot of time before Knight insisted he get his arse to Heathrow.

"Got some identification, laddie?"

"Sure." Snake flashed him his driver's license and waited for the old guy to snap it with his phone.

"Okay. She's parked up in Lot Seventeen. Stay here and I'll get you a site map."

When he returned, he handed him a map and a torch.

"Here, you can borrow this. Just bring it back when you're done. No need to knock. Leave it in the letter box and skedaddle aff." He pointed to the bright red house perched on a stick at the end of the path.

"Thanks. I appreciate it."

"Try not to disturb the other campers. Some of them have to…"

"Yeah, I remember. Early start."

With a huff, Baldy closed the door.

He stumbled along the narrow track leading to Lot Seventeen, one of the smaller sites. No lights. Snake checked his watch. A little after ten. No sign of movement. Odd, he'd never known Sam to go to bed early.

He crouched, hand hovering over the tent flap, and took a breath. Other than finding Sam, he hadn't thought about what he'd say. "Sam. You in there? It's me, John."

No answer. *Tell me, why the hell am I here?* He raised his eyes. Unlike London, stars littered the sky. Far from having an early night, she'd probably taken herself into the nearest village to find company. His eye twitched at the idea of some other man sharing her space, enjoying her smile. No excuses for the possessive bullshit vying for prime position in his head.

"What do you want?" A light shone in the tent. Sam's shadow loomed behind the canvas.

"Er. My plane leaves in the morning." *Shit. She knows that.* "I left before I said a proper goodbye. Thought we might talk?"

"Goodbye."

Got what he asked for—nothing more. "Are you dressed?" His cock certainly hoped Sam lay naked in her sleeping bag. Maybe a little cold. In need of warming up. "It's still early. Fancy a farewell drink at the pub?"

"No. Have a safe flight. I hope all goes well in the Big Apple. Don't forget our postcard. I'll read it to George and Bounce."

"Sam, I…"

"Goodbye, Snake."

When the inside of the tent went dark, any hope he had of seeing her one more time died with the light. Futile, expecting more.

"Bye. I'll write."

"Goodbye."

CHAPTER THIRTY-SEVEN

Click, clack, click, clack. Mis-take, Mis-take. The words sang in Sam's head to the beat of her feet slamming the Manhattan pavement. Over the past year, she must have raised her hands to the sky fifty times a day asking the gods, moon, birds, anything that listened. What the hell whys, sat with the tea leaves in her cup, the crumbs under the toaster, the rain dripping from the roof onto the veranda.

George, on lead, obediently at heel, the bustle of Manhattan's busy worked his nerve as much as it did hers. His huge, sad eyes looked up at her, begging her to get where they were going, faster.

"Hey, lady, watch where you're walking.

A man in a navy wool overcoat bumped her shoulder, knocking her sideways. George growled. "Easy, big boy." It wasn't the first time someone had tried to flatten her today. Too many people, too much traffic.

Sentinel's new headquarters were close to the financial district, plenty of wheeling, dealing knob'eds rushing to work. Briefcase in one hand, a to-go order in the other.

A yellow cab swerved to the curb, two people piled out, slammed the door behind them, and watched their ride stream into the traffic heading uptown.

George tugged on the lead. Taking him for a walk before she dropped him off at Sentinel this morning no longer seemed like a great idea. Uptown, she found it easier to move around. The streets followed the grid, but once they left the East Village, avenues merged, and the streets had names rather than numbers.

The last person she'd asked for directions swore she only had a couple of blocks to go. By her count, she should be there. She pulled George out of the way of the crowd and checked the address. She searched for a sign, a clue. A number might have helped.

Her eyes wandered to the building across the street, her gaze travelling to the second story window. Laugh? She did. A little too loudly for the woman trying her best to keep her chihuahua from attacking George. Cool, as George showed fuck-all interest.

Stuck against the window, a poster of the Statue of Liberty stared down at them. *Hilarious, John.* She'd missed him. A lot. No matter how many whys she shoved in her road, the answer came up the same.

She loved him. Had then, did now, and that was why when he called, she'd said she'd keep George company on the plane. His surprise quickly turned into an itinerary of all the great things he wanted to show her, do with her. Sam fantasised, hoped he had an equally long list of what he'd like to do to her.

George gave himself a shake and grunted. "I hear you. What are we waiting for, ay? Okay, let's go."

From the outside, the Sentinel building kept its original vibe. Red brick, long, skinny windows, and a solid door. Sam huffed at the thought of several flights of walk-up and pressed the intercom button.

"Good morning. How can I help?" asked a female voice, young, sweet.

Sam cleared her throat. "I'm here to see John. John Smith."

"Do you have an appointment?" Still polite, but a tad icy.

"Er. No." She hadn't thought to make it official. She'd messaged John last night that they'd arrive sometime that day. "I've brought his dog." Come to think of it, he hadn't answered.

"Come on up. Fourth floor. I'll tell Snake you're here. Name?"

"Sam. He'll know."

The door clicked open and shut behind them as soon as they were clear of the entry. Sam's jaw dropped. *Wow!* She'd had no idea what to expect. Knight must be doing well.

The builders had renovated and widened the old staircase and must have knocked out a wall because a well-lit hallway led to the back of the building. To her right, *yes*, a lift, *laugh out loud, elevator*. She whispered the word, trying to imitate the Brooklyn accent of the waitress who'd served her breakfast. More difficult than she expected.

George beside her, his head cocked to one side. Sam smiled. The inside of the elevator was slick but serviceable, wide enough to take a few of the big guys and equipment if necessary. Impressive.

The butterflies in her stomach were knocking each other out by the time they reached the fourth floor. The doors opened and again she scraped her chin off her chest. Her gaze skipped the amazing fit-out and torpedoed straight to John.

His powerful energy swamped the entire floor and the blonde leaning against the wall. Arm bent above her head, he leaned in and whispered in her ear.

All the whys ever spoken on the entire planet fell on top of her. Feeling like a complete idiot, she tugged on George's lead. "Come." The receptionist's smile morphed into a frown when Sam handed her the lead and nodded to the end of the corridor. "Tell your boss. Dog delivered." She ran to the lift before the tears pricking her eyeballs could fall. "Bye, George. Love you, boy," she muttered as the doors closed.

"Thanks, Jamie. Remember. No one else need know. She'll be here later. Got it?"

"Yes, boss. I'll arrange everything." Jamie said.

He liked her, a sweet kid. Younger than he normally would think of hiring, but she had mad computer skills and the rest of the team voted yes at her interview. A dog barking put him on alert. "George?" At the sound of his voice, his friend bounded towards him.

"Sam?" He grabbed George's collar and walked to reception, expecting to see her smiling at him. "Who brought him? Where's Sam?" he asked Skye.

"She left. You just missed her." Unlike Jamie, Snake reckoned Skye, the new receptionist, may not last long. He smiled, immediately regretting taking his frustration out on her. "George, stay," he ordered. "Skye, watch him."

He opened the door to the stairwell and raced to the bottom in time to hear the click of the door. "Sam."

Three, maybe four strides later, he made it outside and pulled Sam into his side. "Hey. What's your hurry?" Angry that she'd just dumped George and run, he tried but failed to keep the irritation out of his voice. It had started to rain, and steam billowed out of the manhole covers. "Come back inside." Sam's spine stiffened. Terrified she'd keep walking, he gripped her arm a little harder. "Stay, please."

"You looked busy," she said.

"What. No." Well, okay, he was making sure Jamie had ordered the flowers he'd arranged for Sam and booked the restaurant he planned on taking her to. The last year without her had been hell. Miserable. Tonight, he planned on telling her again he loved her and begging her to give them a chance. An eight-hour flight between New York and London. He'd make it work.

When Sam didn't protest, he shifted his hand to her lower back and guided her inside the building to the seat under the stairs. He took her hands. His hairy mitts swallowed her graceful fingers. "Warm enough?"

"Yes. You?"

"Now you're here. It's good to see you, Sam. I missed you."

"Me, too. Sorry, I mean I missed you, too." Her laugh echoed in the building, filling it and him with all things good.

"How long are you here in Manhattan? Do you have a place to stay? Stay with me." He sounded like an overeager teenager, the words spilling out of him as his lips moved closer to hers.

"Where do you live?" she asked. He couldn't take his eyes off her full, sexy mouth.

"Right here. I live on the top floor." He figured one more breath and he'd be close enough to kiss her.

"Great. I'm happy for you, John. Sounds like you've got everything you wanted."

Her fingers curled underneath his hands. "Not quite."

"Oh?" He could hear her heart racing in her chest. "What's missing?" she sighed.

There you are. His favourite tease. "You." He had to stop with the staccato responses, and he would once he got his breathing under control. Which wasn't happening anytime soon now that Sam's arms had found their way around his neck.

He placed his hands gently on top of hers. "Yes. The gigantic hole in my future is you, Sam." Tears glistened in her eyes. Could he hope they were happy tears?

Sam placed the tip of her index finger on his lips. "Don't even think about laughing at me." She brushed away the unwanted tears from the corner of her eyes.

"Wouldn't dream of it."

"I see a cleaner in your future, big boy. One who's not afraid of large spaces by the look of this place."

"I'm not looking for a cleaner."

"Oh yeah, what then?"

"I'm looking for someone to love. Do you think you might be interested in the job? Loving me?"

"Are you serious?" She wriggled half-heartedly.

Had he gone too far? Scared her out of his arms? "No. I say it to all the people I've interviewed lately just to break the ice."

She thumped him hard on the chest. "You do not."

"Only you can fill the vacancy, Sam. No one else." He cupped her face in his hands and brought her closer.

"I love you, too. I should have said it before. I'm sorry."

Sam couldn't hold back the tears or her smile. Desperate for all of it, he covered her lips with his mouth and poured everything he was into her. "I will do anything to make this work between us. Say the word and I'll tell Knight to find someone else. I won't lie. I'd prefer it if you came here, but it's a lot to ask. I understand if…"

Sam's mouth brushed against his, returned the kiss, soft and tentative at first, as if she were asking permission. She sucked on his tongue, keeping him silent. Drawing him closer. A fire burned in his gut. Her delicious kiss drove the last of the loneliness he'd felt this year away, bathing him in desire and need. They were both breathing heavier when she finally let him go.

"We'll work it out, Sam, as long as you want to be with me as much as I need you in my life, not for the next week, month, or year. Forever. What do you say?"

"Yes."

ABOUT THE AUTHOR

As a child, I had two careers in my mind: Dancer or Professor of English Literature. Dancing won, before I followed my grown-up path. I never lost my love of the written word and stories have stood by me when times were tough and lovers fleeting.

LOVE TAKES COURAGE

Retired now, surrounded by my garden, I can indulge the heroes and heroines in my heart and head, who fight for the love and pleasure we all deserve.

AUTHOR'S NOTE

I hope you enjoyed *Justice* Book Three in the Sentinel Security Series.

I am working on the first in a new spin-off series set in New York City.

Sign up for my newsletter at

www.elizarenton.com

to keep up to date with all news excerpts and freebies. Or find me at

facebook.com/elizarenton or

twitter.com/renton_eliza

How can you help authors if you liked their books? Tell your friends and family.

Consider leaving a review at your favourite online book retailer.

Thank you and happy reading,

Eliza

facebook.com/elizarenton

twitter.com/renton_eliza

www.ingramcontent.com/pod-product-compliance
Lightning Source LLC
Chambersburg PA
CBHW020512120726
47904CB00003B/795